"Muffin's gone," she screamed, tears pouring down her cheeks.

"What?" he asked.

"My dog," she sobbed, rushing past him to go back outside. "Muffin! Muffin!" She continued shouting that one word as she frantically searched her front yard.

He stepped onto the porch, wondering what kind of mess he'd gotten himself into. If he were sensible, he'd head back to the SUV, climb inside and maybe phone this into the police on his way back to the distillery. But what kind of guy would leave a woman alone in a situation like this?

"Hey!" he called, still having no clue of her name. "What's Muffin look like? I'll help you look."

She froze a moment, looking at him as if she couldn't tell if he meant it or not, then, "He's a golden cocker spaniel. About this high." She gestured to just above her knee. "He's wearing a red collar with a gold heart ID tag on it and he has a lot of fur."

"Okay." He nodded and shoved his phone back into his pocket. "I'll have a quick drive around. Why don't you go check if any of the neighbors have seen him?" She appeared more worried about the dog than the house and the culprit looked long gone, so he decided to focus on the mutt first, as well.

"Thank you," she said, her voice choked as she rushed over to the house on her right.

Callum jogged back to his SUV, climbed in and, shaking his head, turned the key in the ignition. When he'd woken up that morning he'd been engaged and planning a wedding. Now it appeared he was single and looking for a stranger's dog. What crazy thin

A DOG AND A DIAMOND

BY
RACHAEL JOHNS

MILLS & BOON

First Published in Great Britain 2016
By Mills & Boon, an imprint of HarperCollins*Publishers*
1 London Bridge Street, London, SE1 9GF

© 2016 Rachael Johns

ISBN: 978-0-263-92011-6

23-0816

Our policy is to use papers that are natural, renewable and recyclable products and made from wood grown in sustainable forests. The logging and manufacturing processes conform to the legal environmental regulations of the country of origin.

Printed and bound in Spain
by CPI, Barcelona

Rachael Johns is an English teacher by trade, a mum twenty-four-seven, a chronic arachnophobe and a writer the rest of the time. She rarely sleeps and never irons. A lover of romance and women's fiction, Rachael loves nothing more than sitting in bed with her laptop and electric blanket and imagining her own stories. Rachael has finaled in a number of competitions, including the Australian Romance Readers Awards. *Jilted*, her first rural romance, won Favourite Australian Contemporary Romance in 2012, and she was voted in the top ten of Booktopia's Australia's Favourite Novelist poll in 2013. Rachael lives in the West Australian hills with her hyperactive husband, three mostly gorgeous heroes-in-training, two fat cats, a cantankerous bird and a very badly behaved dog. Rachael loves to hear from readers and can be contacted via her website—www.rachaeljohns.com. She is also on Facebook and Twitter.

For Beck Nicholas and Jackie Ashenden—
two awesomely talented writers who have been with
me almost from the beginning of this crazy journey
and have become great friends in the process.

Chapter One

"You have arrived at your destination," announced the deep, monotone voice of Chelsea Porter's GPS.

She slowed her car, frowning as she looked up at the sign that loomed above the private bridge to her right: McKinnel's Distillery—Oregon's Best Whiskey since 1977.

Definitely not a place of residence. Perhaps she'd misread the name and address on the client form. Before continuing, she grabbed her cell out of her purse, pulled up her email and checked the details that one Miss Bailey Sawyer had supplied.

Mr. Callum McKinnel, and then what she'd assumed was a residential address in well-to-do Jewell Rock but appeared to be the home of the renowned McKinnel's Whiskey. She didn't drink herself but her grandfather had sworn McKinnel's was the best whiskey in the world. And, like most other members of her family, he'd drunk enough of the stuff to know.

You couldn't live in these parts without having heard of the McKinnel family. Rumor had it the great-great-grandfather of the current McKinnels—and there were a lot of them—had once been a bootlegger. It was his face on the bottle's famous label. Criminal or not, he'd been a handsome devil and, from what she'd heard, his descendants had inherited his good looks.

Now that she was here, staring across the bridge, she couldn't believe she hadn't recognized the name. There'd been an obituary in the newspaper a month or so ago for Conall McKinnel—he'd been the big boss at the distillery for almost forty years until his recent death thanks to a sudden heart attack. Then there was Lachlan McKinnel—a chef who had won numerous awards, he occasionally appeared on local television and blogged his unique recipes online, all while single-handedly raising his disabled son. Callum—whom she guessed to be one of Lachlan's brothers—was probably as close to a celebrity as she'd ever get and her stomach clenched with uncharacteristic and ridiculous nerves.

A horn sounded and she realized she'd stalled in the middle of the road. She waved a hand in apology at the car behind her, turned right and then started over the bridge toward the cluster of rustic-looking buildings in the distance. The lake on either side of her sparkled and she shivered, imagining that at this time of the year it would be icy cold. As she emerged on the other side, the sight before her took her breath away. The building sprawled almost the length of the lake and the word *quaint* came to mind when she looked at it. Although the exterior was brown, there were so many windows that it didn't look dark. The pine trees in the back and the immaculate, stone-bordered garden beds at the front reminded her of a postcard of a holiday resort. When the snow came in a month or so, this place would be magic.

Such a pity she wouldn't have reason to return.

She'd never imagined a place that produced whiskey to be as beautiful and classy as the grounds and buildings that she admired now as she followed the signs to the parking lot around the side. Nope, she associated alcohol with shouting matches, slurred words, bad breath and prayers her parents wouldn't kill each other.

Instead of white lines, the parking lot was marked out with old barrels, which made her smile as she turned off her ignition. Someone, or more likely a whole family of someones, had put in a lot of TLC to ensure this old building continued to sparkle.

Breathing in the crisp cool air that carried a hint of liquor as she climbed out of her car, Chelsea almost forgot to grab the chocolate bouquet off her backseat. Determined not to be distracted by her surroundings, she held her head high as she strode toward the main building, which obviously housed a café if the folks sitting at tables out the front were anything to go by. It wouldn't be long before it would too cold for outdoor dining. She had to sidestep a couple of obvious tourists taking selfies to get inside and contemplated asking if they'd like her to take a photo for them, but reconsidered when she remembered why she was here.

Not to tour or dine or admire the scenery but to be the bearer of bad news to one of the illustrious McKinnels.

That thought made her feel as if she'd swallowed a

brick. *Why?* This wasn't the first time she'd done this. Even before she'd started her business, doing what she was about to do had been a gift. She was determined to get in and get out, because no matter how lovely this place was, it also made her uncomfortable. Chelsea strode the few more steps to the massive, glass-front doors and pushed one open.

If the outside of McKinnel's took her breath away, the inside filled her with warmth as if someone had just wrapped her in a heated blanket. In addition to a number of fall decorations—gourds and pumpkins and whatnot—the walls hung with hundreds of whiskey bottles, black-and-white family photos and old prints related to whiskey drinking. And as she'd predicted, a massive fireplace roared away on one wall. It felt more like she'd stepped inside a cheerful family home than a business. She loosened her scarf and undid the buttons on her coat as she started toward the counter.

As she queued alongside the people waiting to buy or taste whiskey, she looked at the wall behind the counter and smiled as she read some of the many quotes scrawled on a massive chalkboard.

What whiskey will not cure, there is no cure for.

I'd rather be someone's shot of whiskey than everyone's cup of tea.

Too much of anything is bad, but too much of good whiskey is barely enough. —Mark Twain

She might not agree with any of the sentiments but she liked the way all the quotes were in different handwriting as if lots of different people had scribbled their thoughts.

"Hello? Can I help you?"

At the deep voice, Chelsea spun round, tightening her grip on the bouquet as she came face-to-chest with someone. Then she looked up into the face of possibly the best-looking human she'd ever laid eyes on. And not in a clichéd way. Tall, dark and handsome didn't begin to describe him. He was all those things and then some, with an element of something else she couldn't quite put her finger on. And his sea-green eyes just happened to be her favorite color. Although he wore charcoal business pants and a lighter gray shirt with the distillery logo on the breast, his strong, muscular physique and the scar just above his right eyebrow told her he didn't spend all his time behind a desk.

"Are you after a gift or…" His voice trailed off and she realized she'd been openly gaping at him.

Ignoring the strange dizziness that came over her— maybe she'd spun around too fast—she straightened, held her head high and addressed him in her most professional voice. "Hi. I'm looking for Callum McKinnel."

He couldn't be the man standing in front of her because no woman in her right mind would dump someone who looked like *that*. Not even her.

"Then look no more. You've found me." The man's illegally sexy smile didn't falter as he offered her his hand. "And how may I help you?"

He *was* Callum? *Oh, shoot.* Heat rushed to Chelsea's cheeks and she shuffled the chocolate bouquet she held in her right hand into her left, then slipped her hand into his, reminding herself she was here as a professional, not to ogle the produce.

"Can we go somewhere a little more private?" she asked, hoping her voice didn't sound as strained as it felt.

Callum raised a deliciously dark eyebrow and a hint of amusement crossed his lips. "Do we have an appointment?"

She shook her head, trying not to stare at his lips, which were perhaps even more delicious than his eyebrows. Very kissable indeed. "No appointment, but I need to talk to you. I have a message from Bailey, and you might prefer to be alone when you hear it."

At the mention of the other woman, recognition flashed across Callum's face, his smile faded and his eyebrows knitted together. "You'd better come this way."

Before she could ask which way he meant, she felt his large hand across her back and she bit down on her lip to stop from whimpering. What the heck was wrong with her? There were a number of layers between her skin and his; she could only imagine how her body might react if there were not. As Callum led her across the slate-tiled floor, she took a few deep breaths in and out, trying to regain her equilibrium. She told herself this weirdness must be due to where they were, but feared this wasn't actually the case.

"We can talk alone in here," he said as he pushed open a door with a gold sign on it that read Director— Callum McKinnel. The sign looked shiny and new as if it hadn't been in place very long and, when she stepped inside, the office didn't seem at all to Callum's taste.

And how would you know that?

"Take a seat," Callum said, gesturing to a shiny, dark leather armchair as he shut the door behind them.

"It's fine, I'll stand." She rushed her words. "But you might want to sit down."

"That bad, hey?" She couldn't quite interpret Callum's tone, but was glad when he walked around the massive desk and sat in a luxurious leather office chair on the other side. His elbows perched on the desk, he folded his hands and he looked up to her expectantly.

She took a quick breath before launching into her speech. "I come on behalf of Bailey Sawyer." She cleared her throat and continued, forcing herself to look at Callum, despite the fact that looking at him put her all off-kilter. "Bailey acknowledges that you have been in a relationship for five years and that you have both invested a lot of time and energy into each other. She's had a fabulous time with you, but I regret to inform you that she would no longer like the honor of being your fiancée. You're more like a brother or a best friend, and although you had a lot of fun together in other aspects of life, when it comes to sex, the attraction has faded for her."

His eyes widened and Chelsea couldn't meet his gaze, heat flaring in her cheeks. The whole sex thing came up frequently in her line of work—not being physically compatible was one of the top reasons for dumping someone and she prided herself on delivering this news with the utmost tact. She wasn't a prude by any means, but just saying the *S* word in front of Callum McKinnel made her feel like a teenage girl who'd just discovered *The Joy of Sex* in her parents' bedroom.

Jeez, it was hot in here. She mentally gave herself a cold shower as she tried to remember the next part of her spiel. Bailey Sawyer hadn't paid good money for Chelsea to make a mess of breaking up with her longtime boyfriend.

Oh, that's right. She focused. "You are a great guy but Bailey has realized you're just not her type. She doesn't think you want the same things she does and wishes you the best in the future. She thinks one day you could make some woman a very wonderful husband, but she is no longer prepared to come second to your work."

Her heart racing now, Chelsea stepped forward and thrust a bouquet made only of the finest Belgian chocolates across the desk. "These are from Bailey. Your favorite, apparently."

He glared at the chocolates like they were soggy roadkill. "Not anymore, I don't think." He blinked and then ran a hand through his thick, dark hair. "I'm sorry…is this some kind of joke?"

Callum stared at the woman across his desk, waiting for her to say "Smile, you're on *Candid Camera*" or whatever the hell the latest incarnation of that ridiculous show was. She was almost as tall as he was, which was rare in a woman, but she was definitely all woman. Despite the fact she'd just delivered him the news his engagement was over and she was wearing a heavy winter coat, he couldn't help but notice the way her body curved in all the right places. She'd tied her caramel-blond hair back in a high, professional-looking knot, but he could easily imagine what it would look like if she let it all hang loose. Had she even told him her name?

It felt like hours but was probably less than a minute before she replied, "No, I'm sorry, but it's not."

He raised his eyebrows, kinda stunned by this whole bizarre situation and, if he were honest, more than a little annoyed. "What exactly does my relationship with Miss Sawyer have to do with you?"

She cleared her throat again and then glanced back at the door as if contemplating her escape, but he didn't plan on letting her leave until she'd given him a reasonable explanation. "I am a breakup expert," she announced as if this wasn't an alien profession to him.

"A what?" He couldn't help his scoffing tone. Maybe this really was a joke. Bailey liked to think herself a bit of a comedian; then again, he doubted she'd interrupt his work for a laugh. She knew how important the distillery was to him, even more so now that his father had died and he was running the show.

"I'm a breakup expert," she said again. "I handle the difficult task of ending relationships for people who don't feel up to the job themselves."

"You mean gutless people who like an easy copout?" He shook his head before she could reply. "I can't believe what the world is coming to. What kind of person does that?"

"Someone who cares deeply about their partner and feels they may end up staying in an unsatisfactory relationship because they don't want to hurt the other person. Bailey had your best interests at heart when she hired my services."

"I meant, what kind of person does *this* for a job?"

"Oh." Color bloomed in her cheeks and she dropped her chin to her chest, staring at the floor a few seconds before looking up again and crossing her arms. "My reasons for my career choice are no concern of yours, Mr. McKinnel. And now I'm afraid I have another appointment. Good day."

She'd turned and fled the room before he could call her bluff on another appointment. Did she actually get enough of these gigs to earn a living? He stood and hurried after her, weaving through the customers milling in the shop area—the time leading up to midday was a busy one, loads of tourists looking for a place to lunch—but she was fast and he saw no sign of her. Cursing under his breath, he emerged outside just in time to see a little red car reversing out of the lot.

"Dammit." He patted his trouser pocket to check for his keys, then without another thought jogged around the back to his own parked car. Wondering what had come over him but unable to stop himself, Callum started his SUV and screeched after her, narrowly missing a whiskey barrel in his haste. He caught up just as she was turning onto the road in the direction of Bend, the nearest city to Jewell Rock.

As he drove focused on the car in front, he called his sister on speaker phone.

"Good afternoon, McKinnel's Distillery, Sophie speaking. How may I help you?"

"It's me," he barked. "Look, I've had to go out. Can you handle my calls for the next hour or so?"

"Out?" Sophie's disbelief came across loud and clear. "Out where?"

"Never mind. Something's come up. Call me if there's an emergency."

"I may be young and I may be a woman, but I'm more than capable of holding the fort for a couple of hours. Enjoy your mystery rendezvous."

He snorted. Hah! If only she knew what he was really up to. "Thanks, Soph. I owe you one," he said as the traffic lights in front turned amber. Breakup girl zoomed through and, determined not to lose her, Callum pushed down on the accelerator and just scraped through the intersection before the light went red. He checked the rearview mirror in case there were cops, then let out a puff of breath. He could just imagine the look on a police officer's face while they asked him why he'd gone through a red light. Admitting to stalking the car in front could get him into all kinds of trouble and his father would turn in his grave if he garnered any bad publicity that could sully the McKinnel name.

As they drove past the boundaries of town and headed onto the highway toward Bend, Callum glanced at his fuel gauge, hoping he had enough gas to get to wherever she was going. Thankfully it was near full. He supposed he should call Bailey, if only to clarify that the woman he was currently trailing wasn't some kind of lunatic. She'd seemed legitimate but one couldn't be too careful these days.

Bailey *always* answered her phone but today the number went straight to voice mail. "Hi there, you've reached Bailey Sawyer, event planner extraordinaire—leave a message and I'll get back to you soon. Bye."

"Bailey, what the hell is going on? Call me."

He'd been acting on some sort of adrenaline until now, but as he followed the little red car, navigating the country roads between Jewell Rock and Bend, realization dawned on him. What would he tell his mother if his relationship with Bailey had actually ended? She'd been so pleased when he and her best friend's daughter had announced their engagement…and annoyed that they'd taken years to get to the stage of almost tying the knot. This, so soon after the loss of her husband, would devastate her. Anger surged inside him at Bailey and he almost missed the moment when breakup girl turned down a street on the outskirts of Bend.

He slammed on the brakes and swerved to follow. He'd been a teenager with a brand-new license the last time he'd driven this recklessly and he was out of practice. About three minutes later, she swung into the driveway of a little house that looked in dire need of renovation.

Callum parked on the street out the front. Should he confront her now or wait until she was done with the next lucky recipient of her "work"? He waited and watched a moment, but when he saw her unlock the front door and go straight inside instead, he realized she must live here.

In that case... He climbed out of his SUV and beeped it locked, all psyched up to confront her, to demand more of an explanation. And, if he were honest, to tell her what he really thought of her career choice. But his bluster cooled the moment he stepped into her doorway. Either her housekeeping skills were dismal, or while she'd been delivering him the breakup speech, some scumbag had broken into her house. The smashed glass panes on her door indicated the latter.

Standing in the middle of the disarray, she bent down, grabbed some kind of vase off the floor and then spun around and held it as if she were about to hurl it at him. "Stay right there!"

He froze and held his hands up in surrender.

Recognition dawned in her eyes. "You! What are you doing here?"

"I...um..." For once in his life he was lost for words. Now didn't seem the time to pay out on her.

"Never mind." She shook her head, threw the vase onto the couch and headed down a hallway, wailing "Muffin, Muffin!" as she went.

Frowning, Callum stepped inside and surveyed the mess. Whoever had done this had left no stone unturned. What a violation. He dug his cell out of his pocket, about to call the police when she returned.

"Muffin's gone." Tears streamed down her cheeks.

"What?"

"My dog," she sobbed, rushing past him back outside. "Muffin! Muffin!" She continued shouting that one word as she frantically searched her front yard.

He stepped onto the porch. What kind of mess had he gotten himself into? If he were sensible, he'd head back to the SUV, climb inside and phone this in to the police on his way back to the distillery. But what kind of guy would leave a woman alone in a situation like this?

"Hey!" he called, still having no clue of her name. "What's Muffin look like? I'll help you look."

She froze a moment, looking at him as if she couldn't tell if he meant it or not, then said, "He's a golden cocker spaniel. About this high—" she gestured to just above her knee "—he's wearing a red collar with a gold heart ID tag on it and he has a lot of fur."

"Okay. Got it." He shoved his phone back into his pocket. "I'll have a quick drive around, why don't you go check if any of the neighbors have seen him?" She appeared more worried about the dog than the house and the culprit was probably long gone, so he decided to focus on the mutt first, as well.

"Thank you." Her voice was choked as she rushed over to the house on her right.

Callum jogged back to his SUV, climbed in and, shaking his head, turned the key in the ignition. When he'd woken up that morning he'd been engaged and planning a wedding, now it appeared he was single and looking for a stranger's dog. What crazy thing could happen next?

Chapter Two

"Did you find him?" Chelsea asked as half an hour later Callum climbed out of the SUV he'd just parked behind her car.

He shook his head. "I'm sorry." He sounded genuinely so and a prick of guilt jabbed her heart that she'd dumped him without hanging around to offer support. The services of The Breakup Girl included counseling of the dumpee and it wasn't unusual for her to spend up to an hour with the brokenhearted after she'd done the main part of her job. She let her clients' exes pour out their hearts to her, and by the time she'd finished, most of them had decided getting shafted was the best thing that had ever happened to them. As her old friend Rosie often said, some people could cook soufflés that didn't flop in the middle, some people could play a musical instrument and Chelsea's talents lay in the art of dumping people. But she'd failed dismally in being a professional where Callum was concerned; being in the confined space of his office had flummoxed her.

And instead, here he was helping *her*.

"I guess you didn't either," he said as he walked toward her.

She shook her head, sniffing as the tears threatened to fall again. She hated crying and rarely did so—especially in front of other people—it made her feel weak. But there was only one thing in the world that truly mattered to her and that was Muffin, so these were exceptional circumstances. How would she survive if he didn't come back?

"Let's get you inside," Callum said. And before she realized what was happening, she felt his arm close around her shoulders as he ushered her toward her front door. He was so warm, so solid, and she had a crazy urge to lean into him but instead she pulled away and headed inside, conscious of him following behind her. Chelsea was unsure why he was hanging around, but not in the head space to question. She'd barely noticed the mess the first time—so focused on Muffin—but now she hardly recognized her home. Living alone it was easy to keep things tidy as she liked them, but her little house looked as if she'd moved in a year ago, emptied everything she'd owned onto the floor and left it there.

"I don't understand what they were looking for," she said, surveying the mess. It would take her days to clean this up, but her first priority was finding Muffin.

Callum came up behind her. "Probably just kids, but either way, we should call the police before you move anything."

"I need to do up some notices about Muffin and hang them around the neighborhood." She glanced over at her little desk—or rather where her little desk was usually set up in the corner—and promptly burst into tears. They hadn't taken her laptop or her printer but the desk had been upturned, her laptop looked to be broken in two and her printer lay in a number of smashed up pieces.

Callum cursed as he followed her gaze. Two seconds later he was right beside her. "Here." He offered her a crisp white handkerchief. She took it, surprised—she didn't know men still carried such things.

"Thank you," she whispered and then used it to wipe her eyes.

As if a mind reader, he said, "My mom makes me carry it. She says you never know when you'll need one and I'd never admit it to her, but it does come in handy every now and then."

She almost smiled. "I'm Chelsea Porter, by the way. And tell your mom thanks."

"I will. I'd tell you my name but I think you already know it. Can I fix you a drink? A coffee or maybe something stronger? I'd offer you a whiskey but I left in a bit of a hurry and didn't bring any."

Wasn't she supposed to be the one offering him a drink? She shook her head. "Thanks, but all I care about right now is finding Muffin."

And she didn't drink—not that he needed to know that.

"I know you're concerned about your dog," he said, his tone soft and understanding, "so let me call this in to the cops and then I'll help you work out what to do about Muffin."

She sniffed and looked up at him properly. Lord, he was delicious, but she didn't even know him. "You're being very kind to me, considering...considering what I did to you."

He shrugged. "I have two little sisters. I'm used to female hysterics."

She noticed he made no comment on his now *ex*-fiancée. "I can guarantee I'm not usually like this."

His lips curled up at the edges and she couldn't help but smile a little too. "Besides, my mom would have my guts for garters if I left you alone to deal with this."

"I like the sound of your mom."

"She's not bad. But if you'd prefer, I could call a friend to come and be with you."

She *should* tell him that he could go and she would call a friend herself, but the truth was she hadn't made any real friends in her time in Bend. Acquaintances yes, but no one she'd call on in an emergency, and however pathetic it made her, she didn't want to be left alone right now. This burglary had shaken her up, reminded her that no matter how hard she worked to achieve the things she wanted, she still didn't have complete control over her life. "I haven't been in town long enough to make many friends." Then she added, "But you don't have to babysit me. I'm a big girl."

"You *are* tall," he said. "I haven't met many women who are up to my chin without wearing heels, but I wouldn't call you big."

He'd noticed she was wearing flats? She couldn't help being impressed—in her experience most men noticed nothing unless it was naked—and also a little flattered. Which was ridiculous. He'd just been dumped by his fiancée and Chelsea's priority right now was finding Muffin. Her heart rate quickened again and she swallowed, trying to halt another wave of tears.

"But," he continued, hopefully oblivious to her thoughts, "you shouldn't have to deal with this alone. Let me call the police and then we'll work out what to do next." Without another word, he stepped back outside onto her porch and a few moments later she heard his illegally sexy voice on the phone.

She sighed and flopped down onto the sofa, unable to believe this had happened. It felt surreal—Callum whom she'd only just met here helping her, yet Muffin achingly absent. Since she rescued Muffin from a shelter almost three years ago, he'd always, without fail, met her at the door with his tail wagging and his tongue hanging out when she'd returned home. It was true what they said about no one loving you quite as much as a dog did; she'd never had anyone who even came close.

She'd tried to make this house a home by filling it with bright cushions, bookshelves, funky ornaments and life-affirming, happy quotes, but without Muffin, it felt empty.

"A patrol unit will be here as soon as they can," Callum said, coming back into the room.

"Oh, thank you."

He sat down on the other end of the sofa and her belly did a little flip at his proximity. She hadn't had a man in her house for… Well, not since she'd moved to Bend actually.

"Now," he continued, not at all affected by *her* proximity to him, "the police suggested you make a list of what's been taken for when they arrive. They don't want you to move or touch anything, if possible. While you do that, I'm going to call the local vets and animal shelters and give them Muffin's description. Have you got a photo?"

"Um…" She nodded and gazed around the mess, looking for her framed photos, but in the end, gave up and dragged out her cell. "Here," she said after a few seconds of scrolling through photos. The majority of her photos were selfies of herself and Muffin—walking in the park, chilling on the couch—but she didn't want to show Callum those photos. Eventually she found one of Muffin standing on the front porch looking out onto the street at something. It was one of the rare moments that her hyperactive dog had stood still.

"He's a cutie." Callum took her phone to look at the photo and his fingers brushed against hers in the exchange. Something warm and tingly curled low in her belly but she tried not to show it on her face.

"He is." She sighed. "I guess I'll go make that list."

The first call Callum made was to a local security firm, asking them to stop by Chelsea's house ASAP to fix her windows and change her locks. He hoped she had insurance to cover this disaster, but if not, he'd foot the bill—call it his good deed for the day. Then, he called every refuge and vet clinic he could find on the internet in the vicinity of Bend, leaving his cell number as a contact because, as he realized when speaking to the first place, he had no idea what Chelsea's was. Besides, he guessed her contact details were on Muffin's collar, so if anyone found him, they'd likely call her first anyway.

As he was disconnecting the final call, a police patrol car rolled to a stop on the curb. He shoved his cell in his pocket and went over to meet the cops.

"You call in a burglary?" asked cop numero uno as the two officers climbed out of the car.

"Yes, I did," he said, trying not to smirk as he eyed the pair who were each other's opposites in almost every possible way. One was short and fat with gray hair and smile lines around his eyes. The other was tall and thin, looked like he'd gotten his police badge from the toy section in Kmart and wore a scowl on his face as if a mere neighborhood burglary wasn't at all the excitement he'd hoped for when he'd signed up.

"Your place?" asked the young guy.

"No," Callum explained as he led them through the sparse front yard to the house. "It's owned by Chelsea Porter. She's a…" What the heck was she besides a woman who'd walked into his workplace and dropped a bombshell on his world? Or what should feel like a bombshell but after the initial shock didn't make him feel anything much more than annoyed. At Bailey, not Chelsea. "She's a friend," he concluded, deciding the officer didn't need to know their exact relationship as it had no bearing on the case.

They stepped in through the front door to find Chelsea staring at the mess in the living room, a notebook in her hand, a pen caught between her lips and a frown on her face. Even with this expression, she was gorgeous, and the fact he could think such thoughts made him wonder if perhaps he owed Bailey a favor. While he loved her—they'd known each other since they were in diapers and had a lot of fun together—he couldn't deny he'd gotten engaged to show his dad he could settle down. Also because he wanted a family and was traditional in the sense that he believed children should be raised within a marriage. He didn't believe in the type of love his mom and sisters gushed about while watching sappy made-for-television movies, but he did believe any relationship could work if you put in the hard yards.

"Jeez, what a freaking mess," commented the younger man, echoing Callum's thoughts as the two officers surveyed the crime scene.

Chelsea looked up and took the pen out of her mouth.

"Good afternoon. I'm Sergeant Moore and this is Officer Fernandez. You must be Chelsea," said the older officer. "I'm sorry this has happened and I know you probably want to get things cleaned up as soon as possible, so—"

"Frankly, I don't give two hoots about the mess right now," Chelsea interrupted. "Ask me what you need to and then tell me you can help me find my dog,"

"Your dog's missing?" questioned Sergeant Moore.

She nodded.

"And—" Officer Fernandez gestured toward the notebook in her hand "—is that a list of the things that were taken?"

"That's just it." Chelsea glanced down at the notebook as if she'd forgotten she was holding it. "I don't think anything was."

Officer Fernandez frowned. "Except the dog?"

Shock flashed in Chelsea's eyes. "You think they stole Muffin? I just imagined he got scared and ran away."

She sank down onto the sofa and Callum found himself crossing the room to sit beside her. He glared at the young cop.

The older one offered Chelsea a sympathetic smile. "Let's not jump to conclusions. I'll ask you a few questions and we'll go from there."

"Okay," Chelsea whispered, her voice shaky.

The sergeant ran through the usual questions—how long Chelsea had been out of the house, what time she came home, had she touched anything, et cetera, et cetera, et cetera. Callum could see her getting more and more agitated as the questions became more and more repetitive.

"Do you think they could have been looking for something?"

She quirked an eyebrow at the cops. "I earn an honest living, but I haven't got any family jewels lying around if that's what you're insinuating."

Callum couldn't help but smile at her sass.

"Okay. And what do you do for a living?" asked the tall, young cop. The way he spoke made it sound as if *Chelsea* was the one who'd committed a crime and Callum fought the urge to say so.

"I'm a breakup expert," she said, in much the same manner she might say she were a hairdresser or a nurse.

Like Callum had done earlier that day, the officers raised their eyebrows and adopted mutual expressions of confusion at this reply.

Chelsea offered a short explanation. "I break up with other people's partners, via phone, email or in person, so they don't have to do it themselves. But I really don't see what my career has to do with this."

"Hmm…" Sergeant Moore pondered. "Could any of

these men you've broken up with bear a grudge? Could they want to hurt you like you hurt them?"

"First," she said, her eyes sparking, "it's not just men I dump, and second, I am good at what I do. So no, I think that is a highly unlikely possibility. Are we almost finished? While we're sitting here, none of us are out there looking for my dog. What exactly are you going to do to try to find Muffin? Can you register him as missing?"

Officer Fernandez smirked and spoke in a patronizing tone. "Missing dogs aren't actually our area of expertise. I suggest—"

"But," interrupted his superior, "as Muffin may have been stolen he *is* our responsibility. I assure you we will do our best to find him and return him to you and get to the bottom of all this." He gestured around him at the mess.

"Thank you," Chelsea said, standing. She saw the two men to the door and then grabbed a ball cap off a hook on the wall near the door. It appeared to be the only thing in the whole place left untouched. She tugged it down onto her head and was about to step through the front door when she turned back, as if suddenly remembering him.

"And thank you for everything too, Callum," she said. "You've been beyond generous with your help and if there's anything I can ever do to you to repay the favor…"

"Forget it." He waved his hand. "You going out looking for Muffin again?" *Stupid* question.

"Yes. I want to have a thorough search of the neighborhood on foot before it gets dark."

"I'd offer to help," he said, "but someone should stay here and wait for the security guys instead."

Her face fell and it was obvious she hadn't given one thought to her unsecured house. "Oh. No, you don't have to do that," she said quickly. "You've helped enough already."

Damn straight he had and he couldn't really explain why he'd offered, but neither could he just walk away. He liked animals as much as the next guy, but he'd never seen anyone quite so distraught over a dog as Chelsea appeared to be. She really shouldn't leave her house unattended the way it was or someone might come in and loot the place. "My conscience says otherwise. Now go find Muffin. Unless you don't trust me."

She narrowed her eyes at him. "I don't trust anyone, but I also care little about the contents of this house." And with that, she turned on her heels and hurried down the front steps, the sight of her cute ass in her tight business trousers making his gut clench.

Alone and cursing his red blood cells, Callum called his sister again and told her he'd be out longer than he'd first imagined. Although he heard the curiosity in her voice, she didn't pry and for that he was thankful.

His life had suddenly become very complicated, and he wasn't sure he could explain everything that had happened today even to himself.

Chapter Three

Callum glanced at his watch, hoping the security company he'd called wouldn't be too long, and then once again looked around the cottage-sized house surveying the mess. The cops had done their thing—although he didn't think they were taking this burglary as seriously as they should be—so he could start the cleanup without fear of disturbing evidence. Although this wasn't his house, he'd never been the type of guy to sit around and twiddle his thumbs. Putting his phone and keys down on the kitchen counter, Callum pushed up the sleeves of his shirt, wondering where to start. Not wanting to overstep the mark by rifling through Chelsea's possessions, he chose to begin with gathering up the broken glass and other damaged goods.

He found plastic trash bags in a drawer in the kitchen and a vacuum in the cupboard in the hallway.

Taking his time not to throw out anything that looked important or of sentimental value, he went through the house collecting the big bits of unsalvageable debris. On the kitchen table were a few pieces of a jigsaw puzzle. He glanced down and saw hundreds of other tiny pieces scattered on the floor. Collecting them back up into the box took a while and he hoped he'd found them all. Next he righted the furniture that had been upturned in the invasion and put the pieces of her computer back on her desk. As he did so, his gaze caught on a photo—miraculously it didn't appear to be a victim of the carnage—and he realized something that had been bugging him about Chelsea's home since he stepped inside. The one-and-only photo Chelsea had on display was of an old man sitting in a tattered armchair with a teenage girl standing behind him, her arms wrapped around his neck. To him, it seemed almost unfeminine not to surround yourself with photos of memories and loved ones; it was just something he'd taken for granted as part of the female way. Until now.

Without thinking, he picked up the frame and stared down at the photo. The young girl had to be Chelsea, all that unruly caramel-blond hair hanging over her shoulders. Yet, although her mouth was stretched into a massive grin, her eyes weren't smiling—instead they harbored an anxious, unsettled look, exactly the same as the expression she'd been wearing today. He frowned in response and found himself wondering what her story was. Why didn't she have other photos? Was this man her only family? There were all these prints of affirmative quotations on the walls—All That I Seek Is Already within Me, Allow Your Soul to Sparkle, You're Never Too Old to Wish Upon a Star—

as if she were trying to create a safe happy haven, but there was something missing here. Something warm, something real.

A knock on the open front door startled Callum from his reverie. "Hello! Anyone home?" called an overly chirpy male voice.

Callum rolled his eyes. Exactly how many people left the door open if they went out? And if they did, well, they probably deserved to be burglarized. "Yep. Come on in," he called, putting the framed photo back down on the desk and turning toward the front door.

A short but very buff guy, dressed in a tight-fitting uniform stepped inside and raised his eyebrows as he looked around. "Someone sure went to town on your place."

Callum didn't correct him or comment that he'd already tidied up a lot of the mess. He just wanted this man to leave again. Instead, he nodded. "I need you to replace the locks on all the doors, replace the glass that's broken and," he added almost as an afterthought, "can you also install proper locks on the windows?" Chelsea's current locks wouldn't even keep out a small child, and for some reason, knowing what she did for a job, he didn't like the idea of her living in an insecure house. Even he, a relatively levelheaded man, had felt a surge of rage toward her when she'd first "dumped him," so he could imagine there were men out there who might get a little heavy-handed after such mortifying rejection. He didn't like the thought of that one bit.

"No problemo," said the security man, dropping a toolbox to the floor and then stooping to open it. He started immediately, and although he whistled while he did so, he worked quickly and efficiently and of that Callum approved.

While the worker changed the old locks and installed new ones, Callum continued tidying up. The noise of the security man's machine blocked out his whistling and Callum experienced a sense of achievement when he finally switched it off and examined his progress. Callum's mom would be proud—she always harped on about raising new-aged heroes—and Bailey didn't know what she'd lost.

Bailey. He was beginning to wonder if she hadn't done him a favor. She was right—he didn't have the time at the moment to give her what she wanted as all his energies needed to be piped into reviving the distillery.

He simply wished she'd had the guts to tell him to his face.

Callum sighed at that thought. His dad had done a stellar job of pretending everything was okay, but the truth had startled him when he'd finally gotten his hands on the business's books. McKinnel's Distillery wasn't in dire straits but it was pretty damn close. He put this down to the fact his father refused to move with the times, despite the number of other boutique distilleries and breweries that were popping up all around them. Every time he'd raised this issue when his dad had been alive, every time he'd suggested a new idea that could raise revenue, Conall had poohpoohed whatever the latest proposal was and reminded his son who was in charge.

Sometimes Callum couldn't believe he hadn't cut and run from the family business years ago, but the truth was, he loved the distillery almost as much as

Conall had. You had to wonder though whether the stress of declining business had contributed to his father's fatal heart attack.

If only you'd let me help, Dad. If only you'd given me the chance to prove myself.

But Conall McKinnel had been a hard man, almost impenetrable to anyone except his wife, for as long as Callum could remember. Mom put it down to the tragic loss of his twin brother, Hamish, which had happened not long after the two had established the distillery.

"I'm all done," announced the security dude, appearing suddenly beside Callum in the living room and offering him a bunch of shiny, new keys. "You've done a good job of cleaning up here too."

At the other man's tone, Callum almost expected him to give him a pat on the back. "Thanks," he said, referring to the work done, not the compliment. He dragged his wallet out of his pocket. "How much do I owe you?"

The man quoted what sounded like an exorbitant amount, but Callum handed over his Amex without question. "Can you give me a receipt for the insurance company?"

"Sure thing, buddy."

Callum flinched at the term of endearment and bit his tongue, which wanted to say that they weren't "buddies" at all. According to his mom, sisters and even Bailey, he had a tendency to be unnecessarily grumpy. Quite frankly, he thought much of the population had an unnecessary tendency to be jovial.

When the workman realized Callum wasn't the type for idle chitchat, he left, beeping his horn and waving as he reversed out Chelsea's drive. Once again Callum found himself alone at this stranger's house. Standing on her front porch, he looked up at the darkening sky and then down at his watch. Chelsea had been gone a few hours now and he guessed this meant she hadn't found her mutt, but surely she couldn't stay out all night looking. He'd called the shelters, the cops and neighbors knew the dog was missing—what more could she do?

With this thought, he decided to go look for her himself. Callum found a scrap of paper, scribbled down his cell number in case she returned before he found her and needed to get inside her house, then stuck it onto her front door. Ensuring her house was indeed secure, he locked the door, popped her new bunch of keys into his pocket and then jogged toward his SUV. Although he'd grown up in Jewell Rock, he'd never spent much time in Bend and he'd certainly never driven around this end of town.

He drove slowly down the surrounding streets, getting the occasional odd look from locals who wondered who this stranger patrolling their neighborhood was, but the only woman he wanted to pick up was the intriguing Chelsea Porter. A rush of blood shot south at this thought, catching him off balance. He wasn't in the market for a hookup. All he wanted was to get Chelsea home safely, so he could get on with his life.

Finally, he saw her and let out a breath he hadn't realized he'd been holding. Miss Porter was a damn sexy woman and he was defenseless against his pounding red blood cells. *Calm the hell down*, he told them, as he pulled his SUV over to the side of the road and wound down the window.

"Chelsea!"

She turned and blinked at him as if he was the last person she expected to see. Although she didn't speak, her eyes were bloodshot and mascara was streaked down her cheeks. His heart turned over in his chest at the sight.

"You've got new locks on your house," he said, hoping this might give her a lift. It didn't. She blinked as if wondering what that had to do with the price of eggs. "How about I take you home? It's getting dark." Left unsaid was the fact that if she hadn't found the dog by now, it was unlikely she would.

Chelsea shook her head, a few golden locks that had escaped her ponytail swishing across her face in the process. "I can't. Muffin is out here somewhere. All alone. He needs me."

Her desperation told him she likely needed the dog more than the dog needed her. Callum curled his fists around the steering wheel, but refused to let his frustration show on his face. What was he supposed to do now?

"How about you get in…" He leaned over and opened the passenger door. "And I'll drive you around a bit more." Maybe once she was in the confines of his SUV, he could convince her to go home and call it a day.

She looked at him skeptically a few moments, then sighed and climbed into the vehicle. "Why are you being so nice to me?" She asked as she tugged the seat belt over her breasts and clicked it into place. "After what I did to you today?"

"That wasn't personal. Besides, I'm a nice guy," he replied, although the thoughts he was currently having about her breasts contradicted this statement.

She shrugged as if she didn't believe in the fairy

tale of nice guys—smart chick—but at least she was in the car. He didn't need to win her approval, he simply needed to get her home and hand over her keys, so he could leave in good conscience.

As he steered the SUV back onto the road, Chelsea spoke again. "You can take me home and I'll grab my car," she said matter-of-factly. "I'll be able to cover more ground that way."

"It's fine," he said. "Two sets of eyes are better than one. I'll help you."

"Thanks," she whispered, almost too quiet to hear, and then settled back into the seat.

"How long have you lived in Bend?" he asked as they circled her extended neighborhood a few times. So far they'd witnessed two fat cats having it out in someone's front yard and a teenager who was learning to drive reverse into a fence, but they'd seen no sign of her cocker spaniel.

"Just over a year," she said, as if that was the end of the conversation, but stuff it, he was playing chauffeur here and for some bizarre reason wanted to know more. His mom always said he was like a bear with a bee in his bonnet when he wanted something.

"Where was home before?"

She mumbled the name of a suburb in Portland, her gaze never veering from out the window.

"What brought you to Bend, then?" he asked. "Family? A boyfriend?" There hadn't been any signs of either in her house, and he found himself hoping it was because the latter didn't exist. Which was ridiculous. It's not like he wanted to play the part.

She turned her head to glare at him, her nostrils flaring slightly. "Are we playing a game of twenty questions that I don't know about?" Even with bloodshot eyes and all that runny mascara, *especially* with the edge of irritation in her voice, she was gorgeous. Quite simply one of the most stunning creatures he'd ever laid eyes on.

His mouth quirked at the edges. "Sorry. You don't have to tell me anything."

She sighed and crossed her arms over that delicious rack as he kept driving. "My grandfather—the only family that mattered to me—died fourteen months ago and I needed a change of scenery. I had no boyfriend, a dead-end job, no family, so I saw no reason to stay in Portland. I decided to get in my car and drive until something inside told me to stop and put down roots. I had plans to go much farther afield, but something about Bend got to me. Maybe it was the fact that apparently 49 percent of people here own dogs? Besides, I found out Muffin wasn't big on road trips."

He chuckled. Despite being obviously distraught, she had a sense of humor.

"I'm guessing you've lived in these parts all your life," she said, indicating discussions about herself were done.

"Yep. Born and bred in Jewell Rock. I was recently considering spreading my wings a little, but then my dad died and, well, now I'm needed at home. At the distillery." Which was what he'd always wanted—he just hadn't wanted his dad to be pushing up daisies in order to make it possible.

"Were you and Miss Sawyer going to move?"

Truth was, Chelsea was the first person he'd confessed to about the fact he'd been considering leaving the family business. Guilt made his gut heavy at the thought. "We were in discussions," he lied.

Silence reigned a few more moments as they both kept their eyes on their surroundings, then, when they neared a famous chicken fast-food joint, Callum's stomach rumbled so loudly he felt certain Chelsea must have heard it too. He hadn't eaten since breakfast and he guessed she hadn't eaten in hours either.

Without a word, he pulled into the drive-through.

"Hey," she exclaimed, "what are you doing?"

"Ordering us some dinner. What do you want?"

All Chelsea wanted was her dog back and she thought she'd made that perfectly clear, but now that Callum mentioned it, she was starting to feel a little light-headed. Maybe she needed food. Or maybe the dizziness was because of being in a confined space with six-feet-plus of sexy McKinnel. Either way, she found herself asking for a fried chicken sandwich and a serving of french fries. Callum ordered the same, but added some coleslaw. The teenager behind the speaker who took their order giggled ridiculously at the sound of his deep sexy voice.

"Did your mom tell you that you should have veggies with every meal?" Chelsea asked as they waited in front of the window for their food. She thought it kinda cute the way he'd mentioned his mother a few times.

"Something like that." He almost smiled and something inside her quivered so that she had to glance away. Looking out the window made her realize she hadn't thought of Muffin in all of two minutes. Not that she wanted to forget him—she desperately wanted, needed to find him—but Callum had given her a few moments' reprieve from her anxiety.

When their orders were ready. Callum took their food from the teenage attendant and passed it over to Chelsea. The smell of hot, greasy goodness filled the car, making her want to moan out loud. She rarely ate takeout—years of not being able to afford such luxuries had become a habit.

"Let me give you some money for this," she said, snapping back to reality and realizing she was sitting in a stranger's car—a client's ex's car more to the point—and he'd just paid for her dinner.

He waved a hand in dismissal as he drove away from the restaurant. The warmth of the food seeped through the paper bag, making her thighs hot. She inhaled again and her taste buds begged her for a fry, but Callum couldn't eat while driving and she couldn't very well eat hers in front of him.

"We can pull over somewhere a few moments if you like so you can eat," she suggested.

"Or we could go back to your place and eat there." His tone was innocuous and it wasn't that she thought he was about to take advantage, but the idea of eating dinner with a guy in her house was so alien it made her nervous.

"But we haven't found Muffin yet." She hated the neediness in her tone but couldn't help it.

"Look, Chels," Callum began, turning to look at her so that his deep green eyes sought hers and made her skin hot. Or that could simply be the way he'd used a nickname for her, as if they were friends, rather than recent acquaintances. She was loath to admit it, but she liked it. "I know you're worried about Muffin, but we've both searched high and low. I've called every dog refuge in a three-hundred-mile radius of Bend. I think maybe it's time to call it a night. What if Muffin comes home while you're not there?"

And with that one simple question, he got her. The thought of her dog finding his way back to the house and her not being there to welcome him tore at her heartstrings. "Okay." She gave one nod of defeat. "If you could take me home, that would be great."

He gave her a warm smile and turned the SUV in the direction of her place. The closer they got, the more nervous she began to feel. Not nervous that maybe she would never find Muffin, but nervous about Callum McKinnel coming into her house. Granted, he'd already spent a good deal of time there earlier in the day, but this now felt like the closest thing she'd had to a date in months.

Don't be ridiculous, came a voice inside her head. *The man just got dumped by his long-term fiancée.*

Actually you dumped him, said an opposing voice, but she blocked her ears—that was simply semantics. Besides, he likely wouldn't stay long—just enough time to scarf down his dinner and, as he was a guy, that could be merely a matter of minutes.

Ten minutes later, Callum parked in her driveway for the third time that day. Chelsea got out of the vehicle and carried their takeout up the path to the front door, all the while trying to act calm, cool and collected. Callum was a few steps behind her and only when she read the note he'd stuck to her door did she remember he had her new house keys. She spun around and almost slammed right into him.

"Sorry," she mumbled as his hands shot out to steady her.

"Not a problem." That smile again. Quite aside from the fact Callum was a client's ex, as a McKinnel, he was also *way* out of her league.

She swallowed a groan of disappointment as he let her go and then retrieved a bunch of shiny keys from his jacket pocket. Stepping past her, he selected a key and slid it into the lock, then turned it and opened the door to *her* house for her. Bamboozled by his touch, she let him usher her inside and take the lead.

"Shall we eat in the kitchen or do you prefer the couch?" he asked, shutting her door behind them.

Silence echoed around the house, reminding her of Muffin's absence, but in spite of the aching hole in her heart, she couldn't help notice the state of her house. All clean and tidy now, barely any evidence of the burglary. "Did you do this?" She gaped around and then turned her attention on him.

He nodded and shrugged. "Had to do something while I waited for the security company."

No, actually, he did not. He owed her sweet eff all, but for some reason unknown to her, he'd gone out of his way to look out for her today. That Bailey Sawyer needed her head read. Who cared if Callum wasn't *all that* between the sheets? He was kind and thoughtful, not to mention hotter than the sun itself; these traits weren't ones to be scoffed at in a man. All she could think to say was "Thank you."

"You're welcome."

She looked away because she could no longer handle his intoxicating smile. "Let's eat in the living room. It's more comfortable there."

He followed her to the couch, where he sat beside her as she handed out their food. She'd taken a bite into her sandwich before she remembered her manners. Dammit, she wasn't used to hosting guests. "Can I get you a drink?" she asked, putting the sandwich on the coffee table and shooting to her feet. "I've got club soda or cola."

"I'll have a cola, thanks." He smiled again and then sank his teeth into his own sandwich. It was the sexiest thing she'd ever seen in her life. *Maybe I'm the one who needs her head read?* With that thought she scuttled away to the kitchen, wishing it was farther away so she'd have a little more time to pull herself together.

Chelsea opened the fridge, pulled two cans of cola out and pressed one against her forehead, thankful Callum had his back to her. She could see him from the kitchen, sitting back against her couch as if it were the most natural thing in the world. She shook her head—was this some kind of weird dream? Nightmare? Maybe she'd wake up and discover Muffin sleeping by her feet as he always did and find out Callum McKinnel was nothing but a figment of her imagination. Yet the pain when she pinched herself to check this spurred her into action and she carried the cans and two glasses back over to him. No one in her family had ever drunk soda out of glasses—unless the soda was mixed with something stronger, which it usually was—but Callum had a mom who made him carry a hanky, so the glasses felt necessary.

"Thanks," he said as she cracked open a can and poured it into a glass for him. She tried not to drool as he lifted said glass to his lips and took a sip, the thick columns of his neck muscles flexing as he did so.

Right, time to get a grip on reality. She poured cola into the other glass and downed approximately half of it. Although she hadn't eaten since this morning, the butterflies dancing in her stomach put her off eating. She racked her brain for something to say and then remembered how she'd fled from his office without offering her full service.

"I'm sorry about this morning," she said.

Callum raised an eyebrow. "About dumping me?" He made it sound like they'd been in a relationship and she'd ended it.

She shook her head. "Usually after I've delivered a message to someone, I hang around to chat and see if they're okay."

His other eyebrow lifted. "Good customer service? I approve. So why did you not follow through on that promise this morning?"

The way he spoke, the way he looked at her, made her think he knew the reason and heat rushed to her cheeks. "I'm...not...sure."

"It's okay," he said, half chuckling. "I'm not a big talker and Bailey probably did me a favor."

"Really?"

"Sure, I wouldn't want to be with a woman who didn't consider me Mr. Right."

Callum sounded so lighthearted, but she guessed there had to be pain behind those words. She was about to offer to talk about it now, but he asked a question before she could.

"This breakup business? Is it seriously what you do for a living?"

Surprisingly, she detected none of the repulsion he'd had earlier in his tone.

"Yes. Until recently I also waited tables." She named a well-known establishment in Bend. "But it was either hire another employee to take on some of the breakup load or quit my second job. I chose the latter."

His eyes widened. "No offense, but I'm surprised breaking up with other people's partners is such a lucrative profession."

She couldn't help but laugh. "I wouldn't say lucrative, but I take pride in my work and my reputation is spreading. Breaking up is never easy to do. My service is much like hiring someone to clean your house or mow your lawn. Only cleaners and landscapers don't usually offer counseling, as well."

"How many of these gigs do you get a day?"

She did a quick mental tally. "One or two in-person breakups a week—I only offer that service to customers in Bend and surrounding areas, but I do a lot of online work. Emails, et cetera. Follow-up phone calls for the brokenhearted. Business is good enough that I'm thinking of expanding and looking for freelancers to do face-to-face breakups in other areas."

"You learn something new every day." He popped a french fry into his mouth and she ate one, as well. Then he said, "How exactly did you get into this business?"

Chelsea took a deep breath and surprised herself by telling him pretty much the truth. "My best friend, Rosie—she lives back in Portland—actually suggested it. I have this thing where I can't manage to hold down a relationship for long. Rosie believes I'm just dating the wrong guys, but whatever the reason, at about the three-month mark, I always lose interest and we break up. But we always manage to stay friends. So far this year, I've been to five weddings of ex-boyfriends. Anyway, Rosie once joked that I was the queen of breaking up and could do it for a living and then a friend of hers actually asked me to do so. I only did it as a favor, but it went so well someone else asked me to do it. And…"

"The rest as they say is history?"

She smiled as she nodded. "Yes. I'll admit it's not a very common profession but I honestly think I'm doing a necessary service. Do you know how many people stay in bad relationships because they're too scared to get out?"

He shook his head and she guessed he came from one of those perfect families. She didn't know much about the McKinnels, but his father's obituary had definitely painted him as the ideal family man. And Callum had *how many* brothers and sisters? She racked her brain but couldn't come up with the number. It was a lot, anyway, reminding her again what different worlds they came from.

"Well," she said, "it's a lot." Then she said, "Thanks for the dinner. It was good." Hopefully he'd take the hint that it was time for him to leave. That she no longer needed babysitting, even if a tiny part of her wanted it.

He nodded toward her sandwich still sitting on its grease-proof paper on the table. "You barely ate."

"Sorry." She bit her lip. "I'm too worried about Muffin."

He nodded grimly. "Fair enough. I guess I'd better be going." But he didn't make a move to stand— for some unfathomable reason, he didn't appear in a hurry to abscond.

"Thanks for everything," she said, trying to encourage him. She just wanted him gone so she could ignore her hormones and get back to worrying about Muffin.

Callum reached out and wrapped his long fingers around hers, then gave a little squeeze. "I'm sure he'll be okay. You'll find him."

"Thanks," she said again, slipping her hand out of his for self-protection and then standing. If the guys she'd dated before had all been as lovely as him, maybe she wouldn't have felt compelled to dump them.

He stood, as well, and awkwardness buzzed between them. What was the protocol here? This wasn't a date. He wasn't going to kiss her good-night and ask when they could see each other again. Likely they'd never see each other again and tonight would become some distant memory and she would one day wonder if it had ever actually happened.

"Well." He cleared his throat and looked down at her—not many men looked down on her and she liked the thrill it gave her. "Maybe call me when you find Muffin. Just so I know."

She rubbed her lips together, loving the confidence in his voice that she'd find her dog but also joyful at the prospect of an excuse to call him. Her tongue twisted at the thought, so she nodded.

"You'll need my number," he said.

"I think it's on my front door."

"Right…of course it is." He shoved his hands into his pockets. "In that case, good night."

Chelsea followed him out, waved as he reversed out of the drive and then closed the door behind her, the thud echoing around the now empty house. Having Callum here had been so bizarre, it had given her a few minutes' pardon from missing and worrying about Muffin, but now that he was gone, she had nothing left

to do but worry. She retreated to the couch, collapsed
into a heap and wished there was something more con-
structive she could do than cry.

Chapter Four

It was late by the time Callum returned to the distillery and all but the security lights were switched off. He contemplated going home, but he wouldn't be able to sleep without checking that everything had gone okay this afternoon. Although Sophie had a good head on her, his sister was only twenty-six and had rarely been left alone with the responsibility of the office and the tasting room. Sure, they had a couple of employees to help serve customers, but this had always been a family business and they were the ones with their hearts and souls invested in it.

He parked out the front, let himself into the building and then, happy everything looked as it should, he headed into his office where he poured himself a generous shot of bourbon and took a much-needed sip. This had been, without a doubt, the weirdest day of his life and he scratched his head as he leaned back in his chair and thought over it.

Leaving Chelsea shouldn't have been as difficult as it had been. Sure she was hot and sexy as all that, but so were heaps of women. They'd never made him want to look after them the way she had. It felt more like a compulsion than a want.

The sound of the main distillery door opening broke into his thoughts and Callum sat forward, his muscles immediately on edge. Who the hell would be coming in at this time of night?

"Hey, baby boy, it's just me," called a voice he recognized better than his own. A voice that still insisted on calling him "baby" even though he was thirty-five years old and her eldest child. "Mom," Nora McKinnel clarified a moment later, just in case he'd forgotten.

He rolled his eyes, chuckled and prepared himself for something halfway between a lecture and a sympathy speech. "In the office," he called back, as he stood and retrieved another glass from the shelf behind the desk.

His mom appeared in the doorway as he was pouring her glass. She was wearing a pink fluffy dressing gown, a scarf, a beanie, Wellingtons and her cheeks were flushed from the cool outside air. She still lived in the main house, which was a hundred yards or so behind the distillery buildings, with his brother Lachlan, Lachlan's son, Hamish (the second), and his other brother Blair, who'd moved home a couple of years ago after his divorce. Officially Callum lived in a cottage also on the property but he often stayed at Bailey's apartment in town. He guessed that wouldn't be happening anymore. And dammit, he'd have to go collect his stuff.

"Oh, thank God you're okay." His mom rushed at him, her boots thumping against the solid floor, and threw her arms around him. He just managed to put down the bottle in time.

"Why wouldn't I be?" he asked, although he'd already guessed the answer.

She pulled back slightly and looked into his eyes. Hers were a little puffy as if she'd been crying. "I thought you might have…you know…driven off a bridge or drowned your sorrows in the merchandise."

So she'd heard about him and Bailey. How good news traveled fast. "I'm fine, Mom," he said, escaping her embrace and gesturing for her to take a seat and a drink. Perhaps he shouldn't be okay, but he was. Not that she'd probably believe him anyway. Thanks to Bailey, he could guarantee Mom would be fussing over him for weeks.

"Are you sure?" She frowned as she lowered herself into Dad's leather recliner; he'd called it his "thinking seat."

Callum nodded, sat back in his own seat and lifted his glass again. "Damn, we make good bourbon," he said, trying to distract her. Flavor wasn't the distillery's issue, it was the fact that the younger generation of drinkers were into boutique beers instead. He had a few ideas about how to attract them; he simply needed to convince the rest of his family.

Nora took a sip, then, cradling the glass in her hands, nodded. But the expression on her face said he hadn't succeeded in diverting her thoughts. "Marcia called me this afternoon and told me you and Bailey had split up."

Although he knew she wanted him to tell her it wasn't true, he saw no point in delaying the inevitable. "That's right. We decided we weren't right for each other. Better now than later, right?" Not exactly the whole truth, but he didn't think Bailey should take all the blame when she'd been the one with the guts to end it.

His mom sighed and downed the rest of her drink. "I was so looking forward to the wedding after the awful year we've had."

"I'm sorry." He looked down into his glass.

"Is it too much to want another grandchild?"

Here we go. "Of course not," he said merely to placate her. Currently she had two—a granddaughter and a grandson, both his brother Lachlan's kids—but as she herself had seven adult children, she believed this number vastly inadequate.

"I had so much hope for next year with you and Bailey getting married and I'd thought that Mac and Sian would follow soon after. Now all my hopes and dreams have gone up in smoke."

Used to his mother's drama-queen tendencies, Callum tried to offer a sympathetic smile, but she barely paused in her rant.

"Now you and Bailey have followed Mac and Sian instead of the other way around..." Mac had also recently been dumped by his long-term girlfriend. What a sorry lot they were. "Lord knows Quinn can't keep a woman longer than a weekend, or he doesn't want to—either way, I failed dismally with him. Lachlan married a selfish cow, who broke his poor heart, and as much as I adore Hamish, not many women are prepared to become a parent to a special-needs child. Annabel seems destined to mourn Stuart forever." She sighed and took a quick breath. "Why the heck Blair and Claire got divorced is a mystery to us all considering they still live in each other's pockets. I love her like she were my own daughter, but he'll never meet someone else if he stays best friends with her, and Sophie doesn't show any interest in men whatsoever. Do you think she's a lesbian? I have been wondering quite some time if that's the issue."

Callum almost choked on his last sip. "What? No. I don't know. Maybe?" He shrugged. To be honest, he'd never given it much thought. Sophie was almost as much of a workaholic as him and that left little time for dating.

"Not that I would care," Nora said, waving her hands dramatically as she spoke. "Homosexuality runs in the McKinnel family, after all…" She was referring to his father's twin, who'd died before Callum was old enough to remember him. "And I haven't got a problem with lesbians. I just wish she'd open up to me. I am her mother!"

"Yes, indeed, you are." Callum stifled a smile, knowing his mom didn't think this conversation amusing whatsoever. She continued on, lamenting her children's foibles, but his thoughts drifted elsewhere. He hoped Chelsea would find her dog and wished there was something he could do to make sure of it. He wondered how she was coping now she was alone, and once again, his ribs tightened as he regretted leaving her by herself. Maybe he should call and check in on her? But it was late—what if she'd managed to fall asleep and he woke her? They didn't have the kind of relationship where he could phone at all hours; they didn't have a relationship at all. Tomorrow; he'd call tomorrow. And then, goddamn, he remembered he'd given her his number but he hadn't asked for hers.

His mom's heaving herself noisily off the recliner brought him once again back to the moment. "I guess if you're okay, I better head home to bed. Don't stay up too late working though. Promise me? All work and no play makes Callum a very dull boy."

"Are you calling me dull, Mom?"

She came toward him, grabbed his face between her hands and kissed him on the forehead. "You are a number of *D* words, my son—*determined, driven, discerning, droll, dependable* to name a few—but you could never be dull." She frowned a moment. "Is that what Bailey said? Because if it is, my best friend's daughter or not, I'll have to kill her."

Callum chuckled. "Thanks, Mom, and no, Bailey didn't say that." Although she had said he was bad in bed, which irked him, especially since she'd said it to Chelsea.

"Just as well." Nora started toward the door but turned back as she got there. "So if you weren't off plotting your own death, where *have* you been all afternoon and evening?"

He swallowed, not wanting to answer this question for fear he wouldn't be able to explain why he'd gone out of his way to help a stranger. Also not wanting to go into the whole Breakup Girl thing. Such a concept would fascinate his mom and then she'd want to spend all night hearing about it.

"I was checking out some business…stuff," he lied.

She sighed and shook her head sadly, buying this excuse immediately. No doubt she blamed his obsession with the distillery for his split with Bailey; perhaps to a certain extent she was right.

After waving Callum McKinnel goodbye, Chelsea had tried to distract herself with a little TV. She now lay on the couch, mindlessly flicking through channels—something that had always irritated her when her granddad did it—but nothing could take her thoughts away from Muffin. And Callum. Both the couch and the house felt awfully empty without them here.

Missing Muffin she could understand—it had been years since she'd watched TV or gone to bed without his furry body to keep her warm and his heavy breathing as background noise. But missing Callum? What the heck was that about?

She'd known the man less than twenty-four hours and he was head of a freaking whiskey distillery. After the role it had played in her childhood, there wasn't much in the world she despised as much as alcohol, and whiskey, bourbon, whatever you wanted to call it, was one of the worst offenders. Interestingly enough, Callum hadn't smelled of whiskey, and she should know. She'd sat close enough to him in the car and again on the couch to have memorized his unique and delicious smell. Closing her eyes, she tried to conjure it now—something woodsy and sweet. She licked her lips and took a quick breath, then aimed the remote at the TV and switched it off.

Perhaps going into her bedroom where she hadn't been with him, would help exorcise him from her mind. Besides, she needed her sleep so she could continue looking for Muffin first thing. Standing, she stooped to gather their takeout wrappers, empty soda cans and glasses from the table and then took them into the kitchen. Although exhausted, going to bed and leaving such a mess was something Chelsea would never do. Not after a childhood of living with drunks who couldn't care less about hygiene or tidiness.

In the kitchen, she dumped the trash in the can and the glasses in the sink and then her eyes came to rest on a piece of paper on the countertop. It was an invoice for the locksmith. She eyed the price and… *Hells bells!* Was her new lock made of pure gold? Picking up the receipt, she took a closer look, noticing that, not only had the front door lock been fixed, but Callum had also had the back door lock and all her window locks replaced. Without her consent.

Who does he think he is?

She screwed up the paper in her hands, knowing her insurance company would only see fit to pay for a fraction of this. How on earth would she pay him back? Her business made a good living—she managed to pay her bills and tried to put a little aside for rainy days—but she hadn't asked for this! Fury pacing through her, Chelsea turned and stormed into the living room where the piece of paper Callum had left with his contact details now resided.

She snatched it up and was halfway through punching his number into her cell when second thoughts stopped her. She may not have been raised well—manners were always an afterthought used only to get something you wanted in whichever household she lived in—but she knew getting angry at Callum tonight wouldn't be fair. He'd set aside his own pain of being dumped and gone out of his way to help her today. Getting angry at him, although she was furious, would be like a slap in the face.

Instead, she took a deep breath, left the receipt in the room and went off to ready herself for bed. She'd call tomorrow when she'd calmed down a little (and was hopefully a little less physically aware also) and arrange some kind of payment plan. But, as predicted, sleep didn't come easily. Chelsea tossed and turned all night, worrying about Muffin and, much to her annoyance, dreaming dirty thoughts about Callum.

Callum stared at his computer screen, pondering the best time to talk to his siblings about rolling out a rescue plan for the distillery. The ringing of his cell interrupted his thoughts and he snatched it up off the desk, glowering at the unknown number.

He cleared his throat and pressed answer. "Hello, Callum McKinnel speaking."

A pause followed, which made him think this was one of those annoying, automated telemarketing calls. Then, just as he was about to disconnect, a soft voice sounded. "Hi, Callum. It's Chelsea. We met yesterday."

His gut tightened in recognition as awareness flared through the rest of his body. As if he could forget. "Hi." He cringed at the way his voice sounded choked and a tad needy. "Have you found your dog?" That was the only reason he could imagine she'd call him, even though he had secret wishes that she'd called for another reason entirely.

"No," she whispered, her disappointment heavy in her tone. "I went out again first thing. I've called all the vets and shelters again and put up signs around the neighborhood but, nothing so far."

"I'm sorry. But it's still early. I'm sure he'll come back or someone will find him today." He wasn't sure of any such thing—if the intruder had taken Muffin, Chelsea might never seen him again, but he knew better than to say so. "Anything I can do to help?"

"I think you've already helped enough."

He blinked and frowned at her terse tone. "Excuse me?"

"I found the receipt for the new locks." She cleared her throat. "Replacing every one in the house was quite unnecessary."

He leaned forward and rested his elbows on the desk. Was she *mad* at him? "I disagree. In your line of business, you can never be too careful. You should be living in a more secure house. Those old window locks might as well have been bought in a toy department because they'd never keep out an intruder."

"Maybe, maybe not, but my safety *and* my house are no concern of yours. You should have checked with me."

"It's not a problem, I'll pay for them."

"No way. I will pay you for the work, but I'm going to have to do it in a few installments."

He didn't want her money and he resented the tone she'd taken. "As you said, I had the locks fixed of my own accord, so if you can't afford it, don't bother."

"I didn't say I can't afford it." She sounded pissed and that made him pissed. So much for going out of his way to help someone.

"Okay, then. Whatever." Shit, now he sounded like one of his sisters in a mood. "Pay me whenever you can and good luck finding Muffin." He disconnected the phone before she could say anything more, dumped it on his desk and stared at it.

Well, that was a first. He'd never hung up on anyone in his life. Especially not a woman. But something about Chelsea had him doing crazy things. He ran a hand through his hair and groaned, fighting the urge to call her back and apologize.

Chapter Five

"What do you want?" Callum looked up from his desk a couple of days later at Sophie, who was standing in his office doorway glaring at him, her arms folded across her chest.

"A promotion. To win the lottery. Prince Charming to whisk me off my feet. A never-ending supply of cake. But for you to stop acting like a moody bitch for a couple of days would be a nice start."

He leaned back in his seat and held his hands out in surrender. "What's that supposed to mean?"

Sophie stepped inside, closing the door behind her. "Big brother, I know your heart is breaking and all that and Mom said we all need to treat you with extra TLC. But the way you spoke to that customer you just served…" She paused and raised her eyebrows at him. "Not acceptable. I don't want to have to give you a written warning."

He rolled his eyes but thought back to that customer. "She had no idea about whiskey, and I didn't have time to listen to her uncle's life history to find out what bottle she should buy him for his birthday."

"Callum, Callum, Callum…it is our job to *teach* people about whiskey and also to listen. Listening is a skill anyone involved in the selling of alcohol must fine-tune or did you learn nothing from our dear dad?"

"Fine." He sighed. "You're right. I was a little terse with that woman. Sorry."

"You're forgiven. Just don't come into my tasting room and act like such a grump again."

He nodded his acquiescence. Sophie was right, they couldn't afford to lose customers. "Is there anything else?" he asked, when she still didn't make a move to go. Maybe she really did want a promotion; although he wasn't sure how that would work. He guessed he could give her a better title—director of sales and marketing or something—her own office, maybe a gold plaque on the door?

"No, except I just want you to know that I am here if you want to talk. You know…about Bailey and everything. If you ask me it's a crappy time to dump someone, right before Thanksgiving, not long till Christmas."

"It was a mutual breakup."

"That's not the way Bailey tells it." Sophie shrugged. "Look, maybe you should take a few days off to tend your broken heart?"

"What? And leave you in charge?" he scoffed.

She picked a pen up off his desk and hurled it at him.

Grinning, he ducked just in time. "Thanks for your concern, little sis, but I promise you my heart is not broken. I'll be fine. I've been grumpy because of work, not Bailey." Another lie; he'd been grumpy because he couldn't get that woman—that Breakup Girl, Chelsea Porter—out of his head. He'd lost count of the number of times he'd almost called her these past few days to see if she'd found her dog yet.

"What we all need is to sit down and have a proper meeting about our options," Sophie said, switching from sister mode to professional mode. "You know I'm on your side and think your new ideas are fabulous; we just need to convince Mom, Blair and Quinn." Their other siblings, silent partners in the distillery, would go along with whatever the majority decided. That said, Callum had big plans to get Lachlan a lot more involved in the family business, as well.

He nodded. "Do you want to set a date and gather the troops?" Blair and Quinn were more likely to listen to Sophie; as the youngest in the family by three minutes and twenty-seven seconds, she had certain privileges.

"Sure. Consider it done."

Sophie stood up to leave but as she put her hand on the doorknob to open it, Callum couldn't help telling Sophie what his mom had said. "Do you know Mom thinks you might be a lesbian?"

"What?" She spun around, her eyes sparkling at this news.

He merely nodded, amused.

She rubbed her hands together in obvious glee. "I could have a *lot* of fun with this. Thanks, brother dear." And then she opened the door and practically skipped through it.

Callum let out a heavy breath and turned back to

his computer screen, wondering which idea he should push on, or rather *sell to*, his family first. Some of his innovations would require more time and planning, like expanding the restaurant and also starting to grow their own grain; others wouldn't take much to get started but could increase revenue almost immediately. If they acted quickly and launched a McKinnel's Distillery merchandise line, they might even be able to cash in on the upcoming festive season or maybe that was rushing things.

Still, he'd start with that idea. It wouldn't affect Blair in the production department or Quinn in their warehouse as sales would be made in the shop—Sophie's domain—where they already sold their various types of bourbon.

He'd opened PowerPoint to start a presentation for the meeting when his cell rang. Not planning to answer, he glanced nonchalantly at it to see another unknown number. It wasn't Chelsea because, against his better judgment, he'd saved her number after the last time she'd called. But dammit, he was curious and thus snatched it up to answer before it rang off.

"Hello, Callum McKinnel speaking," he barked down the line, irritated by the interruption.

"Hello," came a hesitant voice. "I'm Lee, calling from the animal shelter in Sisters about your dog. Someone found him wandering in a field not far from here and has just brought him in."

His heart shooting to his throat, Callum sat bolt upright. "You've found Muffin? Is he…okay?"

"He was a little ravenous, so we fed him, and a little dirty—he's obviously been living rough for a few days—but aside from that, he's healthy. Would you like to come in and pick him up?"

"Are you sure it's him?" Callum didn't want to call Chelsea with the good news if he wasn't 100 percent sure. "Is he wearing his name tag? He's not actually my dog, he's a…friend's, but there's a contact number on his collar." Probably best if they called Chelsea directly. Probably best if he stayed well clear of the dog and its owner.

"I'm sorry, he wasn't wearing a collar when he was found. But he matches the description you left with us perfectly."

Callum sighed and tapped his pen against the desk. "I'll be there in half an hour."

"We'll see you then," said the woman before disconnecting.

Wondering what the hell had come over him, Callum ran a hand through his hair and stood, grabbing his keys and checking his wallet was in his pocket as he headed out. He went through the tasting room on his way outside and called to Sophie who was counting stock.

"Can you put any calls through to my cell?"

Sophie glanced up. "Where are you going?"

He winked at his little sister. "Taking a few hours for my broken heart. Back soon." And then he left before she had the chance to ask any questions.

Forty minutes later, Callum parked his SUV in the lot at the front of the animal shelter. As he climbed out of the vehicle and strode toward the front entrance, a cacophony of barks, squawks and mewls grew louder.

"Hi, how may I help you?" asked a woman behind a

counter the moment he stepped inside. He recognized her voice as belonging to the person who'd called him.

"I'm Callum McKinnel, here to collect… Muffin." Why couldn't Chelsea's dog have a more masculine name?

"Fabulous." The woman beamed. "I'll go grab him."

As he waited, Callum glanced around the reception area. There were a couple of cages on one wall with kittens inside and across the other side of room, one entire wall was plastered with pictures of animals in need of adoption, all of which looked bedraggled and lonely. Their sad eyes felt as if they were looking directly at him and a lump formed in his throat. He found himself speaking to the photos on the wall.

"Sorry, but I'm not in the market for a pet. I'm rarely home and I wouldn't have the time to walk you."

"You could always adopt a cat," said the woman, startling him as she returned. "They are quite content with their own company for a few hours a day and don't require you to exercise them."

Ashamed to be caught talking to himself, he ignored her words, lowering his gaze to the mutt at her feet. A gorgeous golden cocker spaniel that looked up at him with wide, wary eyes.

"Muffin?" he said, and the dog cocked his ears up slightly. Well, as much as was possible with those long, floppy, furry things. Callum dropped onto his haunches and held out his hand. "How you doing, buddy? Ready to go home?"

The word *home* seemed to win the dog over and he launched himself at Callum, almost knocking him backward as he started licking his face. The animal-shelter woman laughed as she handed him the dog's lead. "Someone's happy to see you."

He'd be even happier to see Chelsea, Callum thought, his heart rate accelerating at the thought. Once he'd signed a few papers and made a donation to the shelter in lieu of adopting half a dozen strays, he and Muffin were finally in his car ready to go. The moment he turned the ignition to start the SUV, Muffin leaped across the gearbox and into his lap, once again slobbering all over Callum's face.

"Buddy," he said, pushing the dog away. "Boundaries."

But it appeared Muffin didn't have such things and somehow Callum managed to drive all the way back to Chelsea's house with her dog sitting in his lap. By the time he arrived at her place, he was halfway to falling in love with the stupid mutt, not that he'd ever admit that to anyone.

"Come on, you," he said, holding tight on the lead as Muffin jumped down from the SUV. He closed the door behind them and they started up the short path to Chelsea's door. Only as he was about to ring the bell did he consider the fact that she might not be home. She could be out, busy dumping some other poor dude. He found he didn't like that idea, and not because of the actual task, but rather because some other guy would be spending time with her.

Shaking his head of that thought, he jabbed his finger into the doorbell. Approximately ten seconds later, the door opened and Chelsea appeared. Their eyes met, and heat washed over him at the sight of her in skinny jeans and a fitted sweater, but she did not seem so happy to see him. Then Muffin yanked forward and assaulted his owner in much the same manner he'd assaulted Callum at the shelter. The annoyance in Chelsea's eyes was quickly replaced with joy and delight as she wrapped her arms around the dog. Tears, he assumed of the happy variety, streamed down her face as she and Muffin reacquainted themselves.

Callum stood awkwardly on the porch, feeling like a third wheel, yet at the same time pretty pleased with himself for reuniting Chelsea with her beloved mutt. Finally, after what felt like a couple of decades at least, she looked up and the smile she gave him almost knocked him off balance.

"Thank you," she said, her tone dripping with genuine appreciation.

He steadied himself on the doorjamb, feeling as if finding this dog was the best thing he'd done in all thirty-five years of his existence. "My pleasure."

"Where was he?" She straightened, but kept one hand caressing Muffin's head. The dog made a sound almost like a cat purring and Callum couldn't blame him. Who knows what kind of noises he'd make if Chelsea ran her hands through his hair.

He cleared his throat. "At a shelter in Sisters. A jogger found him this morning in a field. He wasn't wearing his collar and I didn't know your number the other day when I called all the shelters, so they rang me." Why the heck did he sound like he was trying to explain himself?

"Oh thank God. That must have been the only shelter I didn't call." She looked almost as if she were about to kiss him, but...no such luck. "And thank *you*. Again. I'm sorry I was a little rude the other day when I called. It's just... I'm not good with needing people. I don't like to feel indebted, but that was no reason to be awful to you when you were just trying to help. Can I blame my rudeness on being worried about this boy?"

"What rudeness?" he asked with a smile.

"Thank you. And it looks like once again I'm in your debt. How am I ever going to repay you for re-uniting me with Muffin?"

It was possibly just one of those things people said, but his mind couldn't help conjuring all sorts of ways she *could* repay him. Heat crept to his cheeks and other less visible parts of his body; at least he hoped they weren't visible but with the effect she had on him, who could tell?

"Come to lunch with me on Thanksgiving," he blurted.

She blinked. "Where would we go?"

Jeez, he hadn't thought this one through at all. He'd be ostracized from the family if he didn't show at home for their traditional lunch. Then again, maybe bringing a date would prove to his meddling mother once and for all that he really wasn't too cut up about the whole Bailey thing. "My parents' place. Mom's house now, I guess. You'd be doing me a massive favor as Mom is hell-bent on finding me another girlfriend ASAP. I want to show her I can get my own dates."

She rubbed her lips together. Then, "So this would be a *date*?"

A big part of him wanted to say yes but he didn't want to lead her on. "A fake one, to keep my mother from worrying about me. I'm not ready for another re-lationship yet, but she can't seem to get that into her head." This part was true—he needed to put everything he had into the distillery for the foreseeable future and that didn't leave time for love and romance.

"Oh. Okay. Because I couldn't date a client."

He smirked. "Isn't Bailey technically your client? And is that a yes?"

She shrugged. "You have a big family, don't you?"

"Pretty big, but don't worry, they're not too scary. My little sister hasn't bitten anyone since she was three."

Chelsea laughed at that and he honestly couldn't recall anything ever sounding quite so beautiful. He wanted to tell her a joke and hear that sound again. "Okay."

"Okay?" he asked.

"Okay." She nodded. "It's the least I can do for you after everything you've done for me. But I'll only come if I can bring Muffin. I'm never letting him out of my sight again."

An unbearable urge to kiss her came over him, but he shoved his hands in his pockets instead. "I'm sure that would be fine. We McKinnels love animals, especially dogs."

"Right. Good then." She met his gaze and then quickly looked away.

"Yep. Good." He should make a move but his legs didn't seem to get the message. "I'll pick you up about noon on Thursday, then?"

She nodded. "Can I bring anything?"

He shook his head. "Just yourself. And Muffin of course. Between Mom and my brother Lachlan, we'll have enough food to feed an army anyway."

She smiled and then they stared at each other a little longer. Until it started to get embarrassing. Until he told his legs if they didn't start walking, he'd chop them off. "Okay. Thursday then."

"Thursday," she repeated.

And, before he did something really pathetic, like lean forward and kiss her, he turned and jogged back to his car.

Chapter Six

As Chelsea waited for Callum to pick her up, she nervously paced the length of the front porch with Muffin chasing at her heels, thinking this was some kind of new game. Perhaps he was right, because she had no idea why she'd agreed to go to the McKinnels' Thanksgiving lunch. It was like she'd rolled a dice and it had told her to go, so she'd said "sure, why not?"

But now she was harboring serious second thoughts.

She should have bought him a box of chocolates as a way of saying thanks for finding her dog. Problem was, Muffin was worth way more than a few sweets. It would have to be a very big box to come close to showing her gratitude, and anyway, there was no way she'd have been able to say anything but yes when Callum McKinnel hit her with *that* smile. It was lethal. Especially set in that sexy, short beard thing he had going on. Chelsea hadn't thought herself a fan of beards, but simply thinking about his had all the organs in her body doing gymnastics.

With a sigh, she sank her teeth into her lower lip and stopped pacing. No point in getting all hot and bothered. What was done was done. This was nothing but a fake date and it would pay for her to remember that. Callum had made that 100 percent clear when he'd asked her. And because of Muffin, she'd felt obliged to help out.

Yes, right, you keep telling yourself that's the reason, Chelsea.

A horn sounded and she turned to see a black SUV pulling into her driveway. *Callum's SUV.* Seconds later he jumped down from the driver's side and Muffin flew off the porch and galloped toward him. Chelsea's stomach did a final tumble turn as she forced her hand up to wave. He grinned and waved back as he opened his arms to receive her dog. Stupid, but her throat clogged with emotion as Callum let Muffin slobber all over him, and then, she snapped out of her silliness.

"Muffin! Leave Callum alone," she called as she grabbed her purse and the bouquet of flowers she'd bought for his mother off the porch chair.

"It's fine. We're old friends." He looked over the top of Muffin's head as she approached them and met her gaze head-on. "Isn't this how you greet all your old friends?"

She couldn't help but grin. He had a way of making her feel comfortable and skittish all at the same time. "Thanks for picking me up. Sorry for putting you out. I don't know why I didn't offer to drive myself." Something she'd been wondering all morning, but she'd been so flummoxed by the idea of a date with him—albeit a fake one—when he'd asked, that she hadn't been thinking straight.

"Nonsense." He stood up and Muffin made a tiny pining sound. "That would have made Mom suspicious. A gentleman *always* picks up his date. You look lovely by the way."

She swallowed and her skin slowly caught on fire as he gave a subtle glance up and down her body. "Thanks."

"That color suits you." He was of course referring to the red, which was the predominant color on the dress she'd spent all morning umming and ahhing over. A dress not really practical for the cool November weather but which she'd paired with some leggings and boots to make it more so. The look on his face made any temperature discomfort worth it. She just hoped she wasn't overdressed. Or underdressed. She'd totally forgotten to ask him the dress code for his family lunch.

"Thanks," she said, resisting the urge to pull her winter coat tightly around her. She liked the way he looked at her but it also terrified her. Callum was wearing smart, navy blue jeans and a marled gray crew-neck sweater with the collar of a flannel shirt peeking out the top—a unique combination of smart and casual, with a massive dose of sexiness to boot.

He strode around and opened the passenger side door for her but Muffin jumped up first. They both laughed.

"He's been a little clingy since he came home," she explained. "I think he's scared we might go without him."

"Never," Callum said as Muffin jumped over onto the driver's seat. "In the back, buddy." He tried to encourage the dog to do as he asked, but Muffin refused to budge.

"Maybe we can put these flowers in the back and he can sit with me in the front?" Chelsea suggested. She'd be squashed, her dress and coat would end up covered in golden fur but...anything for Muffin.

"Let's give it a shot." Callum grinned as he took the flowers from her. "Are these for me? You shouldn't have."

"I didn't. They're for your mom, to say thanks for having me to lunch."

"Good move." He winked. "She'll like you." Then, he opened the back door and laid them carefully on the seat.

A few minutes later the three of them were settled in the front of the car—Chelsea in the passenger seat, Callum in the driver's seat and Muffin happily perched on his lap. She'd protested and tried to encourage the dog onto hers, but Callum had insisted it was fine.

"We drove like this all the way back from the shelter the other day," he told her.

She gave in and they started their journey toward Jewell Rock, which was if anything even more beautiful than the picturesque town of Bend.

"Have the police found out anything about your burglary?" he asked.

"No. They followed up on a few names I gave them, but as we suspected, they're pretty certain it's just kids fooling around."

"Little shits." Callum shook his head and Chelsea found her eyes lingering on the way his hands caressed the steering wheel. To try to distract herself from this sight and also in an attempt to alleviate some of her nerves about attending a big family Thanksgiving, she tried to make useful conversation. "So, can you give me a quick 101 on your family?"

He glanced at her with those big soulful sea-green eyes. "101?"

"You know, a quick course in everything I need to know."

"Ah." His smile widened and she wasn't sure it was because of what she'd said or thinking about his family. "Okay. Well, I'm the oldest—but you already know me."

Not as well as she wanted to, but she pushed that thought aside because this was a fake date and everything.

He continued. "Next is Lachlan. He's divorced but has two kids. Hallie lives with her mother in California and Hamish lives with Lachlan and my mom."

Chelsea frowned. "They took a child each in the split?"

"It's complicated. Hamish has cerebral palsy and his mom couldn't handle that he wasn't perfect. It put a great strain on the marriage and when they split, she only wanted to take Hallie with her."

"That's awful." Her eyes watered as she spoke, her heart aching for that poor little boy. She knew all too well how it felt not to be wanted, especially by a mom who should love you unconditionally.

"Yeah, I know. It turns out not all moms have that maternal love-your-child-no-matter-what thing built in."

"No, they don't." Chelsea hoped he didn't hear the

bitterness in her tone. "Lachlan sounds like a good guy though."

"He is. The best…and an amazing chef too. You haven't eaten until you've tasted one of his creations." Callum cleared his throat. "Then there's Blair—he's our head distiller and makes whiskey almost as good as our dad did. Then again, he did learn from the best."

"Is Blair married?"

"Divorced," Callum said. "Only his split was much more amicable. And no kids involved, which I guess helps."

"Hmm."

"What about you?" he asked. "Do you have many siblings?"

"Nope. None." Although she'd always wished differently. Watching endless episodes of *The Brady Bunch* when she was little had made her crave a big warm family of her own. Or rather, a warm, loving family— she had enough aunts and uncles and cousins, just none who wanted her. "Who's next?"

"That'd be Owen, although he's been called Mac since high school. You've probably heard of him."

She hadn't until the last few days when she'd been Googling the hell out of his family. "The soccer player?"

"That's the one. After kicking that own goal against Brazil in the Centennial Copa, which stopped the US making the finals, he's a bit of a mess at the moment. Mom should be putting her energies into worrying about him more than me."

"Is he going to return to soccer?"

Callum shrugged one shoulder. "Who knows? He doesn't want to talk about that, or anything else come to think of it, with any of us. He might not even show up today. Surely, you'd rather talk about something more interesting than my dysfunctional brothers."

She laughed. "Don't you have sisters too?"

He didn't ask how she knew—she guessed he just assumed that everyone knew the McKinnels, which was probably true if you were a local. "Yes, Annabel and Sophie. And they are gorgeous. But don't tell them I told you, or I will have to kill you."

"I bet you're one of those really protective big brothers, aren't you?" she said, trying not to grin from ear to ear. Callum loved his mom, his sisters and her dog… She was heading into danger territory and needed to get a grip.

"Muffin, stop licking my ear. I can't see the road."

Chastised, Muffin desisted, slumping down and falling promptly asleep across the gearbox and the two of their laps. Chelsea absentmindedly fondled his fur, wishing it was just Callum she was spending the day with. In spite of his massive sex appeal, she felt comfortable with him. The thought, however, of sitting around a table with all his siblings made her palms sweat almost as much as it intrigued her. She had no experience whatsoever with big, close-knit families.

"Sorry, I'm probably boring you senseless talking about my family," he said, as if sensing her nerves. "Tell me something exciting about yourself."

She snorted in a quite unladylike manner. "There is absolutely nothing exciting to tell. I am the definition of boring."

"I don't believe that for a second." He paused, then said, "Who is the old man in the photo on your desk?"

A lump formed in her throat making it impossible to answer.

"Sorry. I wasn't snooping that day. I saw the photo when I was tidying up."

"It's okay." The thought of him overstepping boundaries had never crossed her mind; he'd been nothing but kind and honorable in their interactions so far. She inhaled deeply. "That's my grandfather. He died just before I moved to Bend. I lived with him from when I was about fifteen until then. I was his caregiver."

"I see. I'm sorry." He looked at her with an expression that made her heart swell. "You must miss him. What was his ailment?"

She swallowed. "Alcohol."

Awkward silence reigned for a few moments as if Callum didn't know what to say to that. She felt a little bad because her family's alcohol issues weren't his fault; then again, if people like *his* family didn't make their living from alcohol, then others couldn't buy it. They weren't much better than tobacco companies in her opinion.

Finally, he said, "That must have been very hard on you."

"Yes, but he loved me the best he could, so I wanted to be there for him." Being with Grandpa had been far better than living with her parents and then being shifted from one family member to the next, which is what she'd done until she'd finally landed with him. The easygoing mood that had hung in the air while he spoke about his family had evaporated and she racked her brain for a way to get it back. Her fingers in Muffin's fur gave her an idea.

"You said your family love animals. Does your mom have any at her place?"

"Not right now, but there was always at least one four-legged creature hanging around while we were kids."

For the rest of the drive to the distillery, they spoke about the various pets the McKinnels had owned over the years. She loved listening to the anecdotes Callum shared about the scrapes he and his siblings had gotten into with their furry friends and it also relaxed her, so that by the time they arrived at his mom's house, her hands weren't sweating quite so badly.

"Gorgeous place," she said as Callum opened the passenger door for her and offered her his hand. It was warm and he was such a gentleman; she'd honestly thought they were extinct, like dinosaurs. Muffin had already leaped out the driver's side after Callum and was now snuffling around the garden in the shallow layer of snow that had fallen overnight.

She gazed widemouthed at one of the prettiest houses she'd ever seen. Huge, but not showy. It was in the same style as the distillery, which they'd passed on their way in. There was a beautiful swimming pool right out front. She shivered at the way the water glistened icily right now, but in summer it would be lovely.

"Yeah, I guess it is," Callum said, not letting go of her hand as he shut the door behind her. "One of those things you take for granted when you see it every day. Now, you ready?"

No. But it was too late to chicken out, so she nodded and let him lead her up the garden path toward the front door, Muffin bounding ahead of them and then lagging behind when he found something else new to investigate.

The door was flung open a few steps before they reached it and in the doorway stood a middle-aged woman who had to be Nora McKinnel. She was petite and thin, well groomed in bright clothes. When she threw her arms around Callum, Chelsea could see the love in their embrace. Three seconds later, Nora caught her off guard by throwing her arms around Chelsea, as well.

"You must be Chelsea. Callum said he was bringing a *friend.* Any friend of Callum's is always welcome. So glad you could join us."

"Thanks," Chelsea said, flummoxed and a tad uncomfortable in the stranger's arms.

Nora pulled back and glanced down at Muffin who had inserted himself between the two women. "And who is this delightful thing?"

"This is Muffin. I hope you don't mind, but Callum said I could bring him."

"Mind?" Nora's eyes gleamed. "I'm delighted. Come on in, little fella."

Muffin didn't need to be asked twice, he bounded inside, following the noise of conversation and laughter. Nora stepped aside so that Callum and Chelsea could enter, and as he closed the door behind them, Chelsea's gaze lingered on the large, framed, happy-family snap on the wall. Beneath the photo hung a sign: *This house runs on love, laughter and a lot of whiskey.* Funny, the houses she'd lived in as a kid had been pretty much the same, just without the love and the laughter.

Nora followed her gaze. "Not a bad-looking bunch, my tribe, are they? Of course this was taken a few years ago now. We're all a little more wrinkly these days. I think it was taken on the twins' twenty-first birthday." She reached her finger out and touched it on the man that had to be Callum's dad, and Chelsea didn't know whether she could offer sympathies or not. "Anyway, come along. Everyone else is already here."

Nora took her hand and led her down the hallway into a massive country-style kitchen flooded with people, the biggest table she'd ever seen sitting right in the heart of it. As she took in the beautiful decorations on the table that had already been set, the din died down as everyone else stopped talking to look at her. For a few seconds, Chelsea felt like a new exhibit brought into the zoo, but Nora introduced her as "Callum's new *friend*"—again accentuating the *friend*—and everyone rushed forward to greet her, introducing themselves and talking right over the top of each other.

It was hard to hold on to her nerves when they were all so warm and welcoming. She found herself falling immediately in love with each and every one of the McKinnels, although she didn't know how she was going to keep track of them all. Callum took her jacket, asked in her ear if she was okay and then went off to hang it somewhere as the youngest McKinnel said, "You can sit next to me if you want, Chelsea."

She smiled at the boy who looked about ten years old and whose speech was slightly slurred. "That would be wonderful."

He scrambled off his seat and pulled back the chair next to him, crashing it against his own chair in the process. "I'm Hamish," he said as they both sat back down. "Is this your dog?" Muffin had finished doing the rounds and come to sit between them. "I love dogs."

"He sure is. I think he likes you."

"Everyone likes Hamish, don't they, buddy?" Callum said, returning and taking the seat on the other side of Chelsea. The little boy beamed at his uncle's approval, and Chelsea lost another tiny piece of her heart. It had been a mistake to come here.

"Can I get you a drink?" Callum asked, gesturing to the beverage options already laid out on the table. There was wine and beer like at most celebrations but it was a bottle of whiskey, alongside the pumpkin decorations, that took prime spot in the middle of this table. She got the feeling the wine and beer were there more for the benefit of the *non*-family—herself and Blair's ex-wife, Claire, who was sipping a glass of wine. Yes, that situation was weird.

Chelsea shook her head. "I'm fine right now."

Conversation flowed easily around the big table as the family members took turns taking orders from Lachlan, who wore a white apron and gave directions as if they were in a Michelin-starred restaurant. The only person who didn't say much, the only person who'd merely nodded in greeting at Chelsea when she'd arrived, was Mac, who sat at one end of the table nursing a glass of bourbon. He caught her looking at him and threw her a dirty look.

"Can I do anything to help?" Chelsea asked, glancing away from Mac to Nora.

"Don't be silly," said the sister who had introduced herself as Annabel. She had a lovely smile and a face like a pretty pixie, similar but not quite the same as Sophie, her twin. She looked very fit, which was likely down to the fact she was a firefighter. "Guests don't have to lift a finger in this house, do they, Mom?"

Nora smiled and shook her head.

At the mention of guests the doorbell rang and perplexed expressions were exchanged among the family. All except Sophie who shot up from her seat and clapped her hands together. "That'll be my *special friend*," she said, looking at her mother and then winking at Callum as she shot out of the room.

Chelsea leaned close to Callum. "What was that about?"

He leaned even closer and she tried to focus on his reply, rather than the warm, lovely tickle of his breath against her ear. "Sophie's having a bit of fun with Mom," he whispered. "I'll fill you in later."

She shivered at the way he said *later* and then told herself to get a grip. It was simply a figure of speech—fake dates didn't do *later*.

Sophie returned, her big eyes sparkling and her face lit up with a smile as she glanced at the beautiful red-headed girl attached to her hand. "Family," she said, "I'd like you to meet Storie. Isn't she just, something else?"

Once Storie had been welcomed into the fold and fussed over by Nora McKinnel, the food was brought to the table. Granted the McKinnels were a large family, but Chelsea reckoned this feast could feed the entire population of Jewell Rock and half of Bend, as well. At the sight and aromas in front of her, she worried about her taste buds going into cardiac arrest.

Lachlan, obviously in his element, gave a rundown of what he'd made, listing classic Thanksgiving cuisine—such as roast turkey and green bean casserole—as well as contemporary dishes that sounded amazing…well, all except the baked ham with bourbon glaze. She'd be steering clear of that. He seemed particularly proud of his fall harvest squash salad and later, when she tasted it, Chelsea could see why. The man truly was a genius in the kitchen.

"I want to thank you all for coming here today," Nora began before anyone touched any of the dishes. She sighed, a bittersweet smile on her face. "As our first Thanksgiving without your dad, I know it might be hard to find things to be grateful for, but looking around this table at your father's legacy, I consider myself very lucky. You are all my blessings."

Chelsea blushed when Nora looked her way, seemingly including even her. What would it feel like to be loved like that?

"Anyway," Nora continued, bending and picking something off the floor by her feet, "you might need to think a little more creatively when you fill this in this year, but remember, there is always something to be thankful for. I can't wait to read your entries. Callum," she said, looking to him, "can you please say grace?"

He nodded and then reached out to take Chelsea's hand. Hamish took her other one and she followed the family's lead, closing her eyes as Callum led them in Thanksgiving prayer. She'd never been much of a God person but the way Callum sounded when he prayed almost turned her into a believer. She knew his voice would be haunting her dreams—*read, fantasies*—when she closed her eyes that night.

Callum tried to keep his voice normal as he went through the motions of saying grace, yet inside his chest tightened because he shouldn't be the one doing this. Mom had taken Dad's place in welcoming everyone and now he was taking over in the traditional prayer. Everything felt wrong.

"Amen," he finished, unable to recall what he'd actually said and hoping it made some kind of sense. He looked up to see a tear strolling down his mom's cheek and accepted her smile of approval by offering one back. Firsts after the death of a loved one sucked big-time and as his father had only died a couple of months ago, they still had many more to get through. Christmas. His parents' wedding anniversary. Dad's birthday. He blinked, not wanting to think further than today, and then he realized everyone was staring at him in expectation.

"What?"

"Aren't you going to carve the turkey?" Annabel asked.

He shook his head. Feeling the burden of being the head of the business was one thing, but Lachlan, as second oldest, could help shoulder some of the familial responsibilities at least. "I think our esteemed chef should do the honors."

Lachlan was all too happy to oblige and they all watched, mouths watering as he did so. When he was done, it was everyone for themselves as dishes were passed around the table and food served onto plates. Chelsea appeared a little bemused and also somewhat terrified by the way everyone attacked the lunch. Callum smiled, guessing that as an only child she'd never had to fight for her share of much.

"Can I get you a drink now?" he asked Chelsea, gesturing to the wine and whiskey on the table as he realized she was the only person at the table without a glass. Except for Hamish of course; he drank his orange juice from a plastic tumbler.

She smiled but shook her head. "No thanks. I don't drink."

"What? *Ever?*" He hadn't meant to sound so startled and regretted his outburst the second it left his mouth, especially because it drew the attention of his entire family. They all ceased chewing and looked at her.

"Never." Chelsea, crimson rushing to her cheeks, shook her head. "I come from a long line of alcoholics. It's not worth the risk."

Awkward silence descended across the table. Callum could have kicked himself, but his mom did the honors for him, no doubt thinking he should know this about his date.

"Fair enough," he said, reaching under the table and squeezing her hand to show he understood her decision. And strangely he felt a prick of guilt, as if somehow her family's addiction was on him. Which was ridiculous—the McKinnels produced whiskey for people who appreciated good flavor and enjoyed a social drink. It wasn't his fault if some people couldn't hold their liquor. "Can I get you a soda or something instead?"

"Thanks." She squeezed back and then extracted her hand, reminding him this wasn't real. "A club soda would be great."

He stood, went to pour her a drink and was thankful that by the time he returned, chatter had resumed around the table. Claire, who sat across from Chelsea, had engaged her in conversation and they were talking about their favorite chick flicks or something. He'd always liked Claire, from the moment Blair had brought her home in high school, and he had no idea what had gone wrong with their seemingly perfect marriage.

The meal progressed as it always did in the McKinnel household—everyone talking loudly, multiple conversations taking place across the table like multiple games of tennis on one court. Chelsea appeared to be enjoying herself, smiling at the jokes and politely answering all the questions asked of her, not that they were all that personal. The only hiccup was when Mac spoke for the first time in at least an hour and asked how the two of them had met.

She looked to him for clarification and Callum cleared his throat, buying time. "Through Bailey actually. Chelsea worked with her once." And he left it at that, despite the few raised eyebrows. Let them all think what they wanted to think; he was simply glad her presence meant his mom hadn't used the opportunity of having everyone around to harp on about his needing to find another girlfriend if he didn't want to end up old, gray and alone. There was no such thing as letting the grass grow in his mom's mind, at least not when the possibility of grandchildren was involved.

In between the clearing of the main meal and the bringing of dessert to the table, Mom's Thanksgiving journal landed in Chelsea's lap. She shook her head and made to pass it on to him, but Mom objected loudly.

"Oh, Chelsea, you have to fill it in too. It's tradition that whoever eats at this table does so."

Callum knew it was futile to argue.

Chelsea looked uncertain, but then raised the pen and, after a few moments, started scrawling something. He was glad he was next in line as he found himself curious to see what she had written. Normally he wasn't

much of an inquisitive soul—unless it involved work—
but for some reason he wanted to know anything and
everything about her. While eating he'd kept thinking
back to their conversation in the car and wishing he'd
jumped on the chance to ask about her parents, to find
out what had happened to them and why she'd ended
up living with her grandfather.

When she passed him the book, their fingers
brushed against each other. He smiled as he took it
and then looked down at the open page. She had beautiful handwriting. Neat and easy to read yet flowery
at the same time.

I'm thankful for the opportunity to share a meal
with this wonderful family.

Hah! She might not think they were so wonderful
if she spent much longer with them, but her comment
warmed his heart nonetheless. It took him a lot longer
to decide what to write.

*I'm thankful that I'm finally controlling the reins of
the distillery*, seemed in bad taste and would break his
mom's heart. Besides, he wasn't thankful for his dad's
death. He glanced at Lachlan. *Thankful for a brother
who can cook?* Then to Sophie, who was now practically sitting in Storie's lap. *Thankful for a sister with a
sense of humor?* Finally he turned his head and found
Chelsea watching him. He settled on "I'm thankful
for life's surprises and unexpected twists," and then
passed the book to his mom.

She read all the entries, a massive grin on her face.
After the thankful journal came dessert and, once
again, Lachlan had outdone himself with far more

food than necessary: pumpkin and ginger aqua fresca to drink and grilled stuffed caramel apples, pumpkin pie and, the best dish of all, bread and butter pudding with bourbon glaze. Tasting it only confirmed what Callum had been thinking these past few months, and he couldn't contain his excitement.

"I think this could be one of the signature dishes in our new restaurant," he said to Lachlan. "Would you consider quitting your job in town and expanding the distillery's café into something truly special? Sophie and I have been talking and we believe a proper restaurant at the distillery could really take us to the next level."

Sophie gave him a look that said, Is now really the time or place? But he ignored it. Sometimes you had to follow your gut.

Lachlan leaned back in his seat and considered. "A restaurant?"

"You'd be in charge."

"I always wanted my own restaurant. Do you really think the distillery can support one?"

Callum shook his head, speaking honestly. "I'm hoping this restaurant will support the distillery, but it could be really good for you too. Being the boss will give you much more flexibility in your cooking. Say you'll give it some thought."

Lachlan gave a quick nod. "I definitely will."

Quinn cleared his throat. "And do the rest of us get any say in this new venture? If we're struggling, shouldn't we be focusing on what we already do well? Improving that even more? We're supposed to be about whiskey, not food."

"I love the idea," Annabel said. "Lord knows this town needs more good places to go eat."

Quinn glared at her. "You could always learn to cook."

Annabel shrugged. "And why would I want to do that when there are people, like Lachlan, who do it so much better?"

Nora piped up, a tight smile on her face. "As much as I love the distillery, let's leave business to after Thanksgiving, shall we?"

"Sorry, Mom," Callum said, secretly stoked by Lachlan's initial response.

At that moment, Hamish squealed in delight and everyone looked to him.

"Are you feeding that dog under the table?" Lachlan asked, his tone half amused, half reprimanding.

"I love him," Hamish exclaimed, shattering the tension brought on by discussing business at the table.

"That accounts for why he's been so quiet," Chelsea said. "I did think he was being unusually good."

Everyone laughed and then dug into the dessert.

"I can't eat another mouthful," announced Blair later, when only a few crumbs were left on the serving plates. Desserts didn't stand a chance when the McKinnel clan got together.

"Me neither," agreed the twins, speaking as one as they were frequently prone to do.

"Shall we go into the living room and get on with the fun and games?" Sophie added.

All agreed this was a good idea, so, after a joint effort of clearing the table and stacking the first load into the dishwasher, they retreated into the other room.

"Are you a movie or a board-game person?" Callum asked Chelsea.

She looked confused.

"It's our family tradition," he clarified. "Some of us play games and the others watch a movie. The choice is yours. I'll do whatever you want."

She chose the movie and so he led her over to the sofa and tugged her down beside him. It was so easy to pretend she was his date; half the time he forgot it was an act. Muffin collapsed at her feet, also full from lunch and Hamish, still besotted with the dog, sat beside him on the floor at Callum and Chelsea's feet. As usual, Hamish chose the movie—*The Avengers*—and Callum couldn't help but notice and admire the way Chelsea listened intently to his rambling commentary. Although he and Chelsea didn't speak much, Callum found himself playing the part by stretching out and wrapping his arm around her shoulder. She gave him a brief surprised look and then leaned into him and rested her head on his shoulder. It fit there perfectly.

As the credits rolled up the screen, Nora announced, "It's time to Skype Granddad. Quinn, can you go grab my laptop and set it up?"

"Is that your mom's dad?" Chelsea whispered as everyone soon gathered around the coffee table, the computer perched on it, while Quinn placed the call.

"Yep." Callum nodded.

"Where does he live?"

"He's permanently cruising with a bunch of old friends these days it seems. He lived in the cottage here until my grandma died a few years back. He couldn't bear the emptiness and hasn't lived anywhere as such since."

"That's sweet," she said, then added, "in a sad way. If you know what I mean."

"I do." He squeezed her hand again as Granddad's face appeared large-as-life on the screen.

"He's quite a character," Chelsea said quietly to Callum when everyone had taken their turn speaking to the older man. "I can see where you all get it from."

"Are you calling my family eccentric?" he asked, not at all offended.

Before she could reply, bagpipe sounded across the room and she turned her head to follow the sound. There Blair stood, his elbow heaving and his cheeks red and puffy as he played. "Let's just say I don't know many people who can play the bagpipe, but I'd say cool rather than eccentric," she said.

Quinn heard her and came over to butt in to their conversation. In typical Quinn fashion, he flirted. "We are indeed a family of many talents. Well, some of us are—" he dug Callum in the side "—but you've chosen the wrong brother. Callum is as boring as they come. Do you want me to tell you what *my* talents are? Or maybe I could show you?"

"Or maybe you could take a hike." Callum glared daggers at his brother and then whisked Chelsea away.

"Sorry about Quinn," he said when he had her safely across to the other side of the room. "He thinks himself amusing and is the biggest flirt ever."

"I'm sure he's harmless."

Maybe, maybe not. Quinn had flirted with Claire before and after she and Blair got married and still did now that they were divorced. He'd been the same with Bailey—always leaning in to kiss her cheek or say suggestive things, trying to provoke Callum into explosion.

Strangely, it had never bothered him as much when Quinn tried it on with Bailey, but today he'd seen red.

He'd kind of wanted to punch Quinn in the face.

As if his thoughts of Bailey had conjured her into existence, the doorbell rang again. This time Nora flitted off to answer it—more than a little tipsy after her fair share of whiskey—and returned a few moments later with Bailey and her parents, Marcia and Reginald, in tow.

Dammit. What were they doing here?

Of course, Callum guessed the answer. He hadn't told his mom till this morning that he was bringing a date, and she and her best friend had obviously been plotting to get him and Bailey back together. If it weren't for their moms' meddling ways, they'd probably never have become a couple in the first place.

"Who are they?" Chelsea whispered. At the same time Bailey glanced over and saw them alone in the corner.

He swallowed. Talk about awkward. Things were about to get interesting indeed.

Chapter Seven

"As in Bailey *Sawyer*?" Chelsea tried to stop the wild beating of her heart but this was very, very bad. No wonder the woman was now glaring daggers across the room at them. Even if she had been the one to end the relationship, no female liked to think she'd been replaced quite so easily, and so quickly, as well. Chelsea only hoped Bailey wouldn't find out exactly who *she* was. "As in Bailey your ex-*fiancée*?"

Callum cleared his throat and nodded. "Yes. I assumed you two would have met, but I'm sorry. I didn't know Mom had invited her."

Chelsea felt sick—as if she were in danger of losing the massive lunch she'd devoured. "She's beautiful." In fact, Bailey was the absolute definition of perfection in a classic Audrey Hepburn kind of way. The big bright blue eyes that were still staring at them were framed with the longest, blackest eyelashes ever and set in a milky, blemish-free complexion. Ms. Sawyer had perfectly shaped eyebrows and the same could be said about her body, which was neither skinny nor fat. Curvy, that was the word—totally the opposite of the beanpole that Chelsea was.

Deep breaths, deep breaths. It would be fine—she and Bailey had never actually met, they'd only spoken on the phone, so hopefully the other woman wouldn't put two and two together. "She doesn't look very happy to see you with me."

"Hmm." Callum put his hand gently on her arm and gave her a distracted smile of apology. "Look, do you mind if I go over and have a quick chat?"

She found that she minded immensely, a spark of jealousy she'd never felt before kicking up inside her, but she nodded all the same. "I think that would be a good idea." He started to go and she reached to grab him back a moment. "If possible, could you not mention exactly who I am? My business reputation is on the line."

"Of course not."

He strode to the other side of the room where Hamish was currently wrapped around Bailey, offering an exuberant hug. And here Chelsea had been thinking she was special. Torturing herself, she watched as Bailey let go of Hamish and then stepped into Callum's embrace. The hug was quick, perhaps a little uncomfortable, and he kissed her on the cheek in a purely perfunctory manner, but still the action tore at Chelsea's heart.

"This is fun," said a droll voice coming up beside

her. She turned to see Mac, looking on with a bemused expression. "The old and the new under one roof."

"So you do actually speak?" Chelsea blinked at him, trying to feign an apathetic attitude.

"When it amuses me." Mac took another sip from the glass that appeared to be permanently in his hand.

She'd lost track of the number of times he'd refilled it. Strange thing was he didn't have that smell of booze that had permeated her father's and grandfather's skin. And apart from his three-day stubble, he looked like he cared more about his appearance than either of them ever had. He wore his long chocolate brown hair in one of those man buns that were all the rage these days and, although they weren't her cup of tea, Chelsea had to admit that on him, it worked.

She couldn't help herself. "How long were they together?"

"Too long. Maybe since he was two and she was a few hours old."

When Chelsea's eyes widened, he elaborated, amusement twisting his lips ever so slightly upward. "It was practically an arranged marriage between our 'rents. Mom's handling the breakup a lot better than I thought."

Until Bailey's arrival, Chelsea had been enjoying herself far more than she'd imagined possible, enjoying the fantasy that she was part of this world, this family, actually someone Callum might look twice at. But Bailey *looked* a part of this family, as if she belonged here and had only briefly lost her way, and everyone, except maybe Callum and Mac, appeared happy to see her. Chelsea felt like an intruder, standing in the corner with Mac. She wanted to leave and regretted not bringing her own vehicle so she could do so. Wasn't the first rule of first dates to have an escape plan? Not that this *was* a first date, but she should have thought of all the possibilities.

Turning again to look at moody Mac, she considered asking him if he'd drive her home but decided she didn't want to crash at the hands of a drunk driver.

Finally Callum made his excuses to Bailey and her parents and returned to Chelsea. "Sorry," he said, his soulful eyes searching hers. "You okay?"

"Yep." She held her chin high as she nodded. "But I think Muffin is ready to go home. Could you take us now, please?"

Before Callum could reply, Quinn spoke loudly enough that everyone heard him. "Bailey, Callum tells us he has you to thank for an introduction to Chelsea. How exactly did you guys meet?"

And right then Chelsea wished the floor would grow teeth and gobble her up. Bailey looked over at Chelsea, meeting her gaze head-on for the first time, her impeccable eyebrows coming together in a frown. And at that moment Chelsea knew Bailey knew. So much for maintaining her professional reputation. What must Bailey be thinking? That Chelsea took advantage of clients' exes, swooping in to prey on the poor men when they were heartbroken and vulnerable. Not that Callum had seemed either of those things, but perhaps he was a very good actor.

"Um…we have a mutual friend," Bailey said, totally contradicting what Callum had said earlier about them knowing each other through work. She tossed Chelsea a phony smile and then turned her attention back to the game she was playing with Hamish. The

other McKinnels frowned and looked from Chelsea to
Bailey and then back to Chelsea as if wondering what
was going on.

"Muffin," Chelsea called softly, and he awoke from
his post-prandial meal slumber and trundled across to
her. Then she turned to Callum. "I'll go thank your
mom and Lachlan for lunch."

She started across to where Nora was sipping whiskey with her two old friends and could feel Callum and
Muffin following her.

"Excuse me, Mrs. McKinnel? I'm going now, but
I wanted to say thank-you for a lovely lunch. Happy
Thanksgiving." She dared not even glance at Bailey's
parents.

Nora rose from her armchair and pulled Chelsea
into a hug. "It was lovely to meet you. And please,
call me Nora. I hope we'll be seeing a lot more of you
in future."

Chelsea smiled through gritted teeth—she doubted
that very much. Next she said a speedy goodbye to
Lachlan and, although she felt bad escaping without
talking to Hamish, he was still with Bailey so she snuck
out with Callum into the icy, early-evening air.

"Your jacket," he said, when she shivered on his
mom's front porch. In her haste to escape she hadn't
even thought of it and he'd been distracted also. "I'll
just go get it."

"Thanks." She waited on the porch, stooping to hold
Muffin close for warmth and comfort. How lethal could
Bailey's spreading rumors be for her business? Not
wanting to think about that, she forced her thoughts
to the McKinnels and had to admit they weren't what
she'd expected. It was hard to reconcile the warm,

friendly, playful tribe with a family whose name was famous for its world-class bourbon. Each and every one of them had drunk their fair share, yet no one had gotten rowdy or abusive.

"Here you are." Callum's voice was warm as he stepped close to her and held out her jacket. She lifted her arms and slipped them inside. Although she couldn't see his face as he lowered the jacket onto her, she felt his warm breath against the back of her neck and prickles of awareness flared in that spot. She had a crazy urge to turn around, knowing that if she did so, she'd be perfectly positioned to kiss him on the mouth. How she could think such thoughts after what had just occurred inside she had no idea, but it was like her hormones and her brain were two entirely separate entities.

They stood there, glued to the spot a few moments, and then Callum put his hands on her shoulders, before slowly sliding them down her arms and capturing her hands. "Thanks for playing my date today," he whispered right into her ear. It was freezing outside but her insides sweltered. "I'm sorry for Bailey's unexpected arrival."

"It's fine," she lied, her whole body rigid like a statue. What *was* going on here?

"I really enjoyed your company," he continued, still holding her hands, his body still pressed against hers. Her eyes widened as she felt a hardness pressing into her back.

"Yes," he breathed, reading her thoughts, "I don't think my libido got the memo about this being pretend."

She swallowed. What was she supposed to say to that? *How about I give myself to your libido on a platter then?* Her nipples tingled and tightened at the thought—thank God for the cover of her jacket. "Oh," she squeaked.

He chuckled, the sound flowing through her body like hot chocolate through her veins. "*Oh? Is that all you have to say?*"

She turned her head so she could look at him properly. "What exactly…do you…want me…to say?"

He released one of her hands and then lifted a finger to touch her chin. His touch felt soft and hard all at once, exactly how a man's touch should. "I was kinda hoping you might agree to taking this charade a little further."

Her mouth went dry, but she managed to ask, "How much further?" She wanted him to spell it out so she didn't make a fool of herself.

"To your bedroom."

Those three words were like a match against her skin. This would be a gift to herself. An early Christmas present that she very much deserved. Bailey no doubt already thought the worst, so the damage was already done; doing this couldn't ruin her reputation any further. Still, she wanted to set Callum straight—she wasn't about to enter a relationship with a man who made whiskey. "It can only be once. And no one can know. It's bad enough already that Bailey—"

He interrupted before she could finish. "Honey, that's more than fine with me. I'm not looking for a rebound relationship. My priority right now has to be the distillery. And don't worry about Bailey. I'll talk to her. I'll explain I asked you to lunch to do me a favor. She's a good person and she knows Mom so she'll understand. She won't tarnish your name."

Although part of her wondered why he didn't seem that broken up about their breakup if Bailey was such a good person, another part of her didn't much care right now. All that mattered was the desperate need coursing through her. She was crazy, utterly, certifiably insane but she wanted this more than she'd wanted anything for as long as she could recall.

"Okay," she whispered, then leaned forward and pressed her lips against his to seal the deal. His mouth melded to hers, Callum spun her around so their bodies were also pressed against each other. There was no hiding the desire in his jeans and as Chelsea opened her mouth and welcomed his tongue inside, the illicit taste of him fueled her own desperate need even further. He tasted of the sweet desserts he'd eaten but also of what she guessed must be the whiskey he'd consumed over lunch. He hadn't drunk as much as the others as he knew he'd be driving her home, but the taste was still there and she found it strangely appealing. Intoxicating. Surprisingly delicious. Dangerous.

His hand slid down her back, holding her close as he deepened the kiss. Pleasure flowed through Chelsea and anticipation built within her—if her body reacted this way with a simple kiss, she could only imagine the fireworks that would explode once they got naked together. That couldn't happen fast enough.

As if reading her mind, Callum pulled back slightly and she saw heat and desire in his eyes as he spoke. "We'd better make a move, before we make a scene right here on my mom's front porch."

Chelsea gasped and bit her lower lip. She'd almost forgotten where they were; being around Callum affected her senses, primarily her common sense. The sooner she got him out of her system the better.

"Relax," he whispered, smiling down at her as he brushed his thumb against her cheek. "They can't see us out here, but let's get going anyway. I'm tired of sharing you."

More shivers slid down her spine at his words. She nodded, letting him take her hand and lead her over to his SUV. Tired from all the eating and socializing, Muffin didn't object to sitting in the back. He sprawled across the seat and fell promptly asleep, unaware of the sexual tension buzzing in the air around him. Callum drove the whole way back to her place with his hand on her knee, drawing tiny circles on her skin with his thumb. The material of her leggings did little to numb the effects of his touch and by the time they arrived at her house, she was a writhing bundle of need, desperate to rid herself of her clothes and jump his bones.

Alarm bells sounded in her head—getting involved with Callum McKinnel wasn't a good idea on a number of levels—but she ignored them because this wasn't getting involved. This was getting off. Just once.

She almost whimpered when he parked the car and removed his hand to open the door and climb out. He let Muffin out next and although she knew he would come around and open the passenger door for her, she couldn't wait. Didn't want to. As Muffin bounded up toward her little house, Chelsea met Callum in front of the SUV and took his hand, sending another jolt of desire right to her core.

They didn't speak as she fumbled with her key and let the three of them inside, but their eyes spoke volumes. She could almost see the chemistry that sparked between them. Chelsea switched on the hall light, and the moment he shut the door behind her, Callum's hands were on her waist, spinning her to face him again. For a few long moments they stared into each other's eyes and Chelsea found herself admiring his cheekbones. She wanted to touch them, she wanted to touch every little last bit of him.

And then they were kissing. Kissing like she'd never kissed or been kissed before. His hands were in her hair, caressing the base of her neck as his lips and tongue rid her of her ability for rational thought.

Despite his declaration that he wasn't looking for a relationship, Callum didn't rush things. He treated her as if she were a princess, seducing her slowly but at the same time with an urgency that sent her blood racing through her veins. As he dropped kisses along her jawline and down her neck, he moved his hands to her jacket and gently eased it off her. As it thumped onto the floor, he moved his head lower, pressing his lips against the exposed strip of skin just above her cleavage. Her breasts swelled at his proximity and he cupped one in his hand, testing its weight and teasing her nipple through the fabric of her dress. She arched against him, feeling like a wanton hussy but unable to care about anything but acting on the feelings pulsing through her.

"Take my dress off," she whispered and, without a word, he slipped his hand around her back and obeyed. She shivered as the zipper came down and his fingers brushed against her bare skin. He didn't wait for an invitation to remove her bra and she sucked in her breath as he lowered his mouth around one exposed nipple. He circled it with his tongue and desire tugged deep in her core. Need burned there; if he didn't remove her panties next she might actually combust.

Totally attuned to her needs, he eased one hand inside her panties and her knees almost buckled as his fingers touched her in the most intimate place.

"Oh God," she panted as he stroked her toward further insanity. "Bedroom. Now."

"Invitation accepted," he said, his voice a low growl that only made her more desperate. Then he picked her up and she instinctively wrapped her legs around him as he carried her down the hallway and shut her bedroom door.

Callum knew two seconds after he lost himself inside of Chelsea that once was never going to be enough. He just wasn't sure how to broach the subject of wanting more—he'd meant it when he said he wasn't in the market for a relationship right now. Everything he had to give needed to go into reviving the business and he wasn't about to neglect another woman the way he had Bailey. Then again, Chelsea had been the one to suggest only one night—she'd made it perfectly clear that was all she wanted from him—so maybe she'd be amenable to just a little bit more.

"Can I get you a drink or something?" she asked, breaking into his thoughts as she spoke for the first time since they'd tumbled into her bed. She now lay in his arms, her head resting against his shoulder, her fingers trailing across his bare chest, and he didn't want to let her go just yet. He could do with a postcoital bourbon though and hopefully one drink would lead to another and then… And then he remembered she didn't drink alcohol so she wouldn't have any in her house.

"What are you offering?" he asked, his tone a lot more provocative than he'd intended.

"I make a mean hot chocolate. I'll even share my marshmallows with you." And that sounded provocative also, whether she meant it to or not.

He dipped his head and captured her mouth again, kissing her hard. The kiss wasn't the only thing that was hard. A torturous moan escaped her lips as his erection pressed into her stomach and then, instead of going for a drink, she reached down between their naked bodies and curled her fingers around his hardon.

Just once turned very quickly into twice, which was just as explosive as the first time. If not more so. Chelsea took the lead and he watched, mesmerized, as she rode him. It had to be *the* single most erotic thing he'd ever seen. Their gazes glued to each other, they came together in perfect harmony, the sex totally blowing his mind. Callum tried to tell himself this was because he hadn't had any in a while, but that wasn't true. He and Bailey had done the deed on a fairly regular basis, ticking it off on their weekly to-do lists. He hadn't realized that sex had been so perfunctory for them, that their love life had become routine like everything else. But being with Chelsea made him realize just what had been lacking from his previous relationship.

As she collapsed on top of him, her heart racing against his, the heat of their skin slick against each other, he hugged her close and banished all thoughts of his ex from his mind. When they finally recovered from round two, he still didn't want to let Chelsea go. The thought of crawling out of bed and going on his way, never to return, left his heart cold, frozen.

"How about that drink?" he asked, when she finally pushed herself up off him and wiped her brow with the back of her hand. Her breasts hung naked a few inches from his face and desire reared again inside him. He itched to touch and taste some more, but he didn't want to cause Chelsea discomfort.

"The hot chocolate?" She cocked her head to one side and her golden hair fell across her chest. She was prettier than a painting. Her nakedness was far more appealing than anything the pages of a dirty magazine could offer.

"Yes, please." He pinned his hands beneath his thighs to stop from pulling her back down.

"Coming right up." With those words, she rolled over and slid out of bed. He watched as she picked up a robe that was hanging on the end of the bed and tugged it around herself. All very well, but he'd seen every last inch of her buck naked and the image was imprinted on his mind.

"Need any help?"

She smiled over at him and shook her head, peeling a rubber band off her wrist and then capturing her hair into a ponytail. "Nope. I'll be right back."

Good, Callum thought as Chelsea opened the door and Muffin rushed in; she didn't seem in a hurry to throw Callum out and he decided he'd hang around as long as she let him. Who needed sleep anyhow?

As she headed down the hall into the kitchen, Muffin launched himself onto the bed and attempted to lick Callum's face. He wrestled the dog into obedience, and then rubbed his tummy as they both waited for Chelsea's return.

She came back into the bedroom a few minutes

later and smiled at the sight of them in bed together. "Doesn't look like there's much room for me anymore."

"Shove over, buddy," Callum said, nudging the dog to the bottom of the bed and then patting the empty space on the mattress beside him. Chelsea laughed and stepped toward him, two steaming mugs of delicious-smelling hot chocolate in her hands. She stopped at the bed and passed one to him, putting the other down on her bedside table as she climbed back into bed. In a divine act of God, her robe gaped open, giving him the perfect view of her breasts as she settled beside him.

He took a sip, trying to be on his best behavior, when what he really wanted was to kick Muffin out and go for round three. "Hmm, this is delicious. How'd you make it?"

Her eyes sparkled as she wriggled her eyebrows at him and stretched over to get her own mug. "That is my secret, but I'm glad you like."

"Oh, I like very, very much," he said, taking another sip.

She licked her lips. "Tell me about Sophie," she said, leaning back against the headboard. "Why did she wink at you when she went to meet her girlfriend?"

He chuckled at the recollection. "I told you our mom is a mad-keen matchmaker. She won't rest until all her babies are happily married off and having babies of their own, but for some reason she thinks Sophie is a lesbian. Of course Sophie thinks this is hilarious and has decided to play along."

"Ah I see. So Storie isn't her girlfriend?"

"No. I don't know where Sophie picked her up but I think their act was pretty damn convincing, don't you?"

Chelsea nodded and then met his gaze. "As convincing as ours?"

"Probably not quite," he said, reaching out and wiping away a little chocolate smudge on her top lip. She rubbed her lips together and the heat between them flared again. Maybe now was the time to broach... What exactly did he want to ask of her? A fling or an affair sounded salacious and he didn't want to cheapen her in any way, but neither could he bear the thought of walking away. Of never having her legs wrapped around him again.

"What happened with your parents?" he asked, biding his time and also hoping he didn't scare her off.

She took her time replying, as if deliberating whether or not to do so at all. "What do you mean?" she asked eventually.

"You said you lived with your grandfather starting when you were fifteen. I assumed you meant on your own or did your parents live with you, as well?"

She shook her head and stared sadly into her mug. For a moment he regretted prying, not wanting to cause her any pain. "They died. In a car accident when I was eleven. My father was driving and he'd also been drinking, as he usually was. I was only lucky I wasn't in the car, I guess. It was a total wreck, they both died on impact."

"I'm sorry," he said, reaching out to place his hand against her thigh; this time to offer comfort not sex.

She shrugged. "These things happen."

"Maybe," he agreed, "but they still suck. Who'd you live with between when they died and when you moved in with your grandfather?"

"Who *didn't* I live with, more like. I was shipped

from relative to relative, but no one really wanted me. I think the only reason they didn't give me to Granddad in the first place was that he was almost as much of a drunk as my parents, although he was a happy drunk, unlike my mom and dad who were violent with each other and whoever was around after a few drinks."

Oh God. His heart went out to her. She spoke with such detachment but he could see through her bravado to the hurting little girl inside. His family might have its faults, but he'd never been made to feel like a burden on any of them. Sure his dad had pushed him to achieve his best, but he'd always known this was down to love and wanting the world for his kids.

"No wonder you don't drink," he said.

"Yes." She sighed. "Although your family appear to be able to have a few drinks without yelling and screaming at each other."

"We have plenty of screaming matches, don't you worry," Callum said, "but we respect whiskey too much to abuse it. My dad taught us all that whiskey, any alcohol really, should be drunk and appreciated with good friends. Drinking should be a social event, not something you come to rely on."

She nodded. "You must miss your father a lot."

"It's complicated," he admitted. "Of course I'm devastated that he's gone—so many times I think of things I want to tell him and then realize I can't—but I have to admit, it feels good to be able to follow my ideas and dreams for the distillery. Dad didn't see that if we are to survive, we need to expand and move with the times. He thought making good whiskey was enough."

"And Quinn agreed with him, is that right? I sensed

a little tension between the two of you about the distillery today."

"There's always been tension between us. Of course I love him as I do the others, but we've always rubbed each other the wrong way and I don't think he has the same passion about distilling that Blair, Sophie and I have. It's like he's doing it because he doesn't know what else he wants to do with his life."

"What's his job again?"

"He manages the warehouse, fills orders from suppliers. Most of my ideas will have no effect on his role whatsoever, except that we'll hopefully turn over more whiskey, which in turn means he might earn a better living. I think he objects simply because he can. Anyway, enough about Quinn. I don't want to bore you."

"You're not. Honestly. I must admit, I find big families fascinating. I'd also like to hear your ideas for the distillery."

"Really?"

When she nodded, Callum didn't hold back. He told her about his thoughts for expanding the simple café they currently had into a restaurant, about wanting to have more McKinnel merchandise for sale, about the possibility of introducing a white-dog label and also how he'd recently spoken to an agent about buying some nearby land and actually starting to grow their own grain.

"Do you know anything about farming?" she asked.

He smiled. "Not the first little thing, but I am an expert at delegating. I'd hire someone to oversee that side of things."

"Pity," she said, a twinkle in her eyes as she smiled

back at him, "I think you'd totally rock a flannel shirt, a pair of denim overalls and a big floppy straw hat."

He raised an eyebrow. "I think you're confusing farmer with scarecrow."

She laughed. "Maybe." Then she said, "Have you thought about hosting events at the distillery? Like weddings, birthday celebrations and such. You've got the room for it and your surroundings are so beautiful that I'm sure it could become a very popular venue option in Jewell Rock."

"No, I haven't," he said, the idea already taking root. "What an awesome suggestion." He leaned over and kissed her on the lips to show exactly how much he appreciated it.

"If that's what I get for making suggestions," she said when they finally broke apart, "I'll keep them coming."

"Please do."

They spent the next hour or so—Callum lost track of time—talking and fooling around. He'd never been one to chat much postsex, but sitting in bed doing so with Chelsea seemed like the most natural thing in the world. He enjoyed her company as much as he did her body, and that was saying something.

When Muffin roused at their feet and scooted toward the bedroom door, their bubble of bliss broke. "Dammit," Chelsea said, scrambling after him, "I haven't taken him out for his evening wee."

Callum glanced at his watch as the girl and her dog hurried out of the room. It was much later than he'd imagined—early hours of the morning later—and he should make a move. He didn't want to overstay his welcome, and spending the night had certain connotations. Reluctantly, he climbed out of bed and dressed again.

He found Chelsea outside, standing on the porch, shivering in her robe while Muffin did his business on the grass in front. Every cell in his body wanted to step right up to her and pull her into his embrace to warm her, but he resisted, because if he did so, he wasn't sure he'd ever be able to leave.

And Chelsea Porter was exactly the kind of distraction he didn't need right now.

Instead, he cleared his throat. "It's late. I guess… I'd better be going." He hesitated because although his head told him this was the right move, all his body wanted was to jump back into bed with her.

"Oh. Okay." She turned to meet his gaze, surprise in her eyes, despite the fact they'd agreed this was only going to be one night. *One time.* It was on the tip of his tongue to suggest they arrange another rendezvous, but he simply couldn't bring himself to do so. Whatever way he phrased it, a proposition of the kind he had in mind sounded tawdry. Chelsea didn't deserve to be cheapened in that way. It would be much better to leave things at one mind-blowing night.

Still, this left him with the dilemma of how to actually leave. Should he kiss her goodbye? Seemed stupid to be deliberating about such a thing when they'd already been intimate. In the end, he shoved his hands in his pockets, gave a curt nod, said thanks and then strode over to his SUV and climbed inside, cursing himself as he slammed the door behind him.

Chapter Eight

"Thanks?" Chelsea whispered into the cold darkness as the lights of Callum's SUV disappeared into the night. She shivered and pulled her robe tighter around her, but it did nothing to warm her up. What exactly had she expected him to say? Not that she'd had many one-night stands—tonight, with Callum, brought her total to one—but she guessed the goodbye part was always awkward. Then again, it was better than having to give him the breakup spiel three months down the track when the shine wore off their relationship as it would inevitably have done.

She sighed and called softly to Muffin, not wanting to wake the neighbors. The dog obeyed and once they were both back inside in the warmth, she locked the door behind them.

It was long past midnight, but Chelsea felt wide-awake. Wide-awake but also deflated after what was undoubtedly the best night of her life. She shook her head, wondering if Bailey had been speaking about the same man when she'd said their sex life wasn't the best. Not that she wanted to think about Bailey, because doing so reminded Chelsea that what she'd just done was not only unprofessional but that to Callum she was likely nothing more than rebound sex.

She sighed. But it hadn't only been the sex— although that was off the Richter scale, toe-curlingly amazing—it was everything about Callum, from the way he smiled when he looked at her to the passion in his voice when he spoke about the distillery. In spite of her own feelings toward alcohol, she could have listened to him talk all night. If the insides of her thighs weren't a little raw from being up close and personal with his beard, she would think the last few hours had been a dream. The kind of dream where you woke up and then wanted to fall immediately back asleep. Of course, you never could, and even if you did manage to, the dream had always been lost.

She headed back into her bedroom and picked up their empty mugs, deciding it would be a good idea to erase all evidence that Callum had ever been here. She would pretend it was a dream after all. In the kitchen, she dumped the mugs in the sink, turned on the tap to rinse them and then, out of the corner of her eye, noticed the voice-mail light flashing on her home phone. Without thought, she stretched over to press Play and then frowned at the strange noise that drifted out into her otherwise silent house. She stilled, the little hairs on her arms lifting as she listened.

Is that heavy breathing?

Before she could be certain, the message ended, but another followed almost immediately. "I'm watching you. Don't think you can get away with what you've done."

Chelsea gasped at the sinister tone and then instinctively glanced around the kitchen, checking that she was alone, aside from Muffin who'd put himself to bed in her room. She shivered, now thankful that Callum had insisted on getting all her locks changed. What would be even better was if he'd stayed the night, if he were still here to protect her against bogeymen or crazed stalkers or whoever had left those messages. She immediately retracted this thought—disgusted with the neediness in it. She didn't need a man to keep her safe—she'd looked after herself practically since she could walk—but perhaps she should mention these calls to the police. What if they were related to the burglary?

At this thought, her whole body trembled, and once again she racked her brain for anyone who might want to harm her. Coming up blank, she took a deep breath. Perhaps the two things were unrelated? But that didn't necessarily make her feel any better.

It was late now but she'd called the number Sergeant Moore had given her and left a message. Then, unsettled by the thought of someone wanting to harm her, she double-checked that every door and window was securely locked—*thanks, Callum*—before retreating to her bedroom with Muffin to attempt slumber. She doubted she'd get much sleep with the fear rippling through her, but when she climbed into bed, thoughts of a possible psycho battled with the scent of Callum on her pillow and the raunchy acts of the evening on replay inside her head. Chelsea's body ached in places she'd forgotten existed and she couldn't decide what was worse—fear of a stranger or the fear she might never feel as alive as Callum made her feel tonight ever again.

Callum rubbed a hand over his beard and stared at his computer screen. It was taking him much longer than it should to get through his morning emails and what did it matter anyway? Most of the country took the Friday following Thanksgiving off as an extra holiday and so he doubted anyone would read his replies until Monday morning, but he figured trying to work might keep his mind off Chelsea.

Realizing he'd read the same line of the same email ten times and still had no idea what it said, he pushed back his seat and wandered out onto the tasting floor. Perhaps a walk in the garden would clear his head. He'd had a late night and, despite not drinking since lunchtime, he'd woken with a hangover from hell. He left the office and walked through the tasting room, which was open with a skeleton staff due to the long weekend.

"You look like you haven't slept for a month," Sophie said cheerily as she polished the American oak bar where potential customers could taste their wares.

"Just a night," he replied, heading for the door.

"Can't you keep up with your new woman?" Sophie teased. "Must be getting old, big brother. I've heard there's something you can take for that."

He glared at her, channeling a little of Mac's perpetual grumpiness. "Not a conversation I'm having with my little sister. Call me if we get an influx here and I'll come help you with tastings."

"Okeydoke." She gave him an irritating little finger wave and he went out through the side door in the direction of the actual distillery. He didn't think Quinn would be working in the warehouse today, so he was surprised to see the door open. Deciding that maybe he could try to win Quinn over to his ideas one-on-one rather than waiting until the family meeting, Callum was almost at the door, when Bailey came out, her eyes red as if she'd been crying.

"You okay?" he asked, instinctively reaching out to touch her arm. They'd been officially together five years and friends long before that; it was hard to break the habit of looking out for her. "What's going on?"

"Nothing." She blinked. "I was just…" She shook her head. "It doesn't matter. How are you? Do you think we could talk? I feel like I could have handled our breakup a lot better."

By handling it yourself? He swallowed this response and nodded.

"Sure." He wanted to talk to her about Chelsea anyway. "Want to come into my office or would you prefer to head over to the house and have a coffee?"

"Your office will be fine."

He nodded and escorted her back to the main building. It wasn't that late, but she'd been in the McKinnel world for decades, so he offered her a bourbon and she accepted, downing the entire contents of the glass in a few seconds. They both opened their mouths to speak at the same time:

"I want you to know I never wanted to hurt you," Bailey said.

"I wanted to talk to you about Chelsea," Callum said.

Then they frowned in unison.

"You're not serious about her, are you?" Bailey asked.

He shook his head, because that *should* be the truth, even if he felt his conscience calling him a damn liar. "No, of course not."

Last night with Chelsea had been better than anything he'd experienced in as long as he could remember, but could he trust those feelings right now? He'd been one half of a whole for a long time and he came from a big family—he was used to having people around him. Maybe he'd reached out to Chelsea, simply because he couldn't bear another night of going home alone.

Bailey raised a clearly skeptical eyebrow as if she could see right through him.

"I'm sorry," he said, "I never would have invited Chelsea if I'd have known Mom had invited you. You know what she's like. When she heard we broke up, she was devastated, and to get her off my back, I asked Chelsea if she'd be my date for Thanksgiving."

"You two must have had quite the chat when she… you know, ended things for me."

Bailey sounded accusatory and he was about to say that he'd never have even met Chelsea if she'd done her own dirty work, but she spoke again before he could. "Anyway, it doesn't matter. I should have talked to you myself, but I thought if I did, I might chicken out?"

"What do you mean?"

"You're a wonderful friend, Callum, and I don't want to lose that. Our families go way back. I enjoy your company and I love you but I'm not *in* love with you."

He nodded, understanding because, now she said

it, he realized that was exactly how he felt about her, as well.

"For a long while," she continued, "I've been trying to convince myself that all that was enough. I wasn't sure I could actually go through with ending things, even though I thought it was the right thing to do, so that's why I hired Chelsea. To make sure I did it. Mom thought I was insane breaking up with you and maybe I am but…"

"No." He shook his head. "You were right to do what you did. I think we both know that. You deserve a lot more than I can give you and getting married to keep our moms happy…"

"I know." She half smiled. "Not the right reason at all." She sighed. "Why does love have to be so damn complicated?"

There was something in the way she spoke about love that made him think she wasn't talking about him and something in her eyes made him ask a question he'd never considered before. "Was there another reason you broke up with me?" he asked, finding the idea didn't bother him as much as he thought it would; he was simply curious. "Another man perhaps?"

The way she glanced down at the ground told him all he needed to know.

"Who is he?" he asked.

She shook her head. "It doesn't matter. He doesn't feel the same about me anyway." Then her face crumpled and a sob escaped her mouth. "I'm sorry, Callum, I never meant to hurt you."

"It's okay." And he found he meant it. Not that he liked the idea of being cheated on, but he knew that no one strayed if they were already where they were meant to be. "And, Bails, if this guy doesn't realize how lucky he is to have your love, then he's as big an idiot as me and he doesn't deserve you either."

She half sobbed, half laughed.

"You deserve a good man," he continued, "I'm sure you'll find the lucky Mr. Right very soon. Just be patient."

She sniffed, wiped her nose with the back of her hand and nodded. "Thanks for the drink, Callum. I guess I'll see you round."

"About Chelsea," he said, hoping his voice didn't crack on her name.

"Yes? What about her?"

"You won't tell anyone about her coming over for Thanksgiving, will you? She really was just doing me a favor, and I wouldn't want to hurt her professional reputation."

Bailey stared at him a few long moments, her gaze penetrating. Then, finally, she nodded. "I won't say a word. You have my promise on that."

"Thank you. I'm glad we had this conversation." He didn't want things to be awkward with them going forward. "Our families will always be friends and I hope we will too. We were good as friends."

She smiled, then came around his desk, leaned down and kissed him on the cheek. "We *are* good as friends."

As she turned to leave, he remembered one more thing. "Can I come around tonight to collect the last of my things?" He'd grabbed some of his stuff from her apartment the day after the breakup but there were still some books, CDs, that kind of thing. They'd never officially moved in together, but had rather lived a little at her apartment and a little at his cottage.

"Sure. I'm going round to Mom and Dad's for dinner, but you can let yourself in. Do you think you can bring over anything of mine left at your place?"

He nodded.

"Cool. And then leave your key on the kitchen table." She'd brightened considerably since he'd run into her outside, and he was glad they'd had this conversation.

"I will. Goodbye, Bailey."

"Goodbye, Callum."

His listened as her high heels click-clacked down the corridor and then, determined to focus on the business and forget about women, he turned back to his computer and threw himself into work.

For the next few days, he barely left his office and every time his mind drifted to Chelsea—as it was irritatingly prone to do—he added another task to his to-do list, reminding himself where his priorities lay. If he were to bring McKinnel's back from the brink, he needed to focus and resist the ridiculous urge to pick up his phone and call Chelsea. An urge almost as strong as the one to take breath.

With Sophie's collaboration, he drafted a five-year plan for the distillery with areas left where Mom, Blair, Quinn and the others could add their ideas at the meeting. He felt ready to wow the unbelievers in his family and take McKinnel's Distillery into the twenty-first century.

In addition to introducing merchandise—stuff like glassware, tea towels, hats and T-shirts, which he'd delegated to Sophie to organize—his number one priority was a start on expanding the restaurant and for that he needed to get Lachlan on board. He could hire any old chef but Callum believed having a McKinnel in charge of the restaurant would enhance their family-run image. People liked that stuff, especially journal-ists, whose attention he was hoping to attract with the new ventures. They could do with all the good publicity they could get. He also hoped to lure Mac into helping with the expansion of their current café space. In ad-dition to being a superstar with a soccer ball, Mac had a talent for building things and Lord knew he needed something to focus on now that he'd quit playing pro-fessionally.

On Wednesday, almost a week from the day he'd left Chelsea in the early hours of the morning, it was with all *this* forefront in his mind, that Callum drove into Bend to meet Lachlan for a late lunch. They'd arranged to meet at a café in the Old Mill District, rather than the fancy restaurant Lachlan currently worked at so the owner wouldn't hear them plotting. As he climbed out of his SUV, he looked over and did a double take at the sight of Muffin sitting outside the front of the café, his leash looped around a fire hydrant. At least he thought it was Muffin, but maybe he was hallucinating. He'd certainly been imagining Chelsea all over the place. Twice in the last few days he'd gone out to the tasting floor and mistaken a customer for her.

Trying *not* to think about her was almost as bad as thinking about her.

He strode toward the dog, half hoping he'd see Chel-sea inside the café, half hoping he wouldn't.

"Hey, buddy." He stooped to ruffle the fur on Muf-fin's head and the dog leaped about like a total lovable lunatic. No doubt about it, there was no welcome so wonderful as that of a dog; maybe he should detour via that shelter on his way home and adopt one. Something big like a German shepherd that would require a ton of exercise—running with it could help burn off the pent-up tension that had set up residence inside him these last few days. A dog would also keep him company on lonely nights and likely be less stress than a woman. This thought led him into the café, but the moment he spotted Chelsea it evaporated. His heart caught in his throat and muscles all over his body locked up at the sight of her sitting at a table with *another* man.

A bell above the door sounded, announcing his arrival and Chelsea looked up. Her mouth opened and color rushed to her cheeks; she held his gaze that fraction too long before blinking and then turning back to her date. That thought sent his blood racing, but then he realized that she could simply be in the middle of one of her professional breakups. Even still, Callum couldn't help the rush of jealousy that hit him like an actual physical blow.

He stood in the doorway like a total idiot, glancing around for his brother, wishing they'd chosen someplace else to meet. They lived in the same damn house for goodness' sake, but Lachlan had a strict rule about not taking his work home. All his free time he spent with Hamish.

Speak of the devil. A hand landed on his back and shoved him forward right into the café. Lachlan spoke far too loudly. "Hey, bro, isn't that your new girlfriend over there? Who's the dude?"

Callum met his brother's gaze, glowered and then hissed, "She's not my girlfriend. Just a...*friend*." He almost choked on the last word, like it were a fur ball in his throat.

"Sorry. My mistake." Lachlan didn't sound apologetic in the slightest. "You guys seemed pretty tight at Thanksgiving. Do you want to go talk someplace else?"

While that might be a sensible move, Callum couldn't bring himself to leave. He hadn't expected to see Chelsea today, and now that she was only a few feet away, he couldn't keep his eyes off her. "No, this is fine. Shall we sit?"

Lachlan nodded and the two of them crossed over to a table in the corner. Unfortunately—or perhaps fortunately—his brother sat first, taking the seat with a direct view of Chelsea. Ignoring the disappointment in his gut, he sat down and pulled out his iPad, ready to hit Lachlan with some of his ideas about the restaurant.

Lachlan glanced down at the menu. "Are you hungry? I think I might just grab a coffee."

"Coffee will be fine," Callum replied; he didn't have the mental coordination to eat and talk to Lachlan with Chelsea a few yards away, whose presence was a major distraction.

A waitress arrived and Lachlan ordered for them both. Then he looked directly at Callum. "Before you start, I just want you to know I love the idea of opening a proper restaurant at the distillery and I'm 99 percent on board."

"What's the 1 percent that's holding you back?" Callum asked.

"I want full control."

Callum raised an eyebrow. "That's it?" He chuckled, feeling as if a weight had been lifted off his shoulders.

"I mean it," Lachlan said. "I know you're struggling, trying to get everyone behind some of your ideas, but I have complete faith that you can turn the distillery around. I don't want McKinnels to die a slow death. I believe a restaurant will help immensely, but not if everyone feels they have to put their mark on it. We all need to stick to what we do best."

Callum nodded. "I completely agree. Just one thing—I don't know how we'll convince him, but I'd like to try to get Mac involved in building the extension. I'm worried about him. It's not good to sit around all day doing nothing. The guy needs purpose in his life."

"You're just scared he'll drink all the profits if he doesn't snap out of his funk."

"Damn straight I am," Callum said, resisting the urge to twist his head to see if Chelsea was still with that guy.

Lachlan smirked. "She's still there. The poor dude looks quite cut up, though. I wonder who he is."

"She's dumping him," Callum said, before thinking better of it.

"What?" Lachlan frowned, disgust flashing across his face. "So you're dating a woman already in a relationship?" His ex-wife had betrayed him before she left and he couldn't abide cheaters.

"No. I told you, we're not dating and she's not dumping him because of me. She's dumping him on behalf of someone else."

"Whoa!" Lachlan leaned back in his seat and held up his hands. "You've lost me."

Callum inhaled in frustration and quickly filled Lachlan in on Chelsea's bizarre career, so they could get on with what they were supposed to be talking about. As predicted his brother thought this both surprising and hilarious.

"So let me get this straight," Lachlan said, his voice thankfully low enough that only Callum could hear. "Bailey hired Chelsea to dump you and then you hired her to pretend to be your date?"

"I didn't hire her and it doesn't matter. We're not here to discuss Chelsea."

"Thank God Mom thinks I'm a lost cause when it comes to relationships, and I don't have to go to the extremes you do," Lachlan said, shaking his head.

Callum thought about just how far he'd gone with Chelsea the other night. And then he succumbed to the burning need to turn his head to look at her. His chest tightened as she stood, her caramel hair swishing across her back as she offered the poor man a sympathetic hug, patted him on the arm and then started out of the café. She didn't look at Callum and something inside him squeezed. Was she annoyed? Was that how things were going to be between them? He wanted to be a good memory, not one she regretted. Feeling bad about the way he'd left things the other night, he suddenly needed to apologize more than he needed oxygen.

He shoved his chair back and stood, barely even flinching as it scraped against the floor, sounding like nails scraping down a blackboard. "Be right back," he said to Lachlan, and then he turned to hurry after Chelsea, almost bumping into the waitress as she carried over their drinks.

"Sorry," he apologized and then hightailed it out of there.

Chelsea was speedy, and by the time he stepped out of the café, she'd unlooped Muffin and was striding down the sidewalk like she couldn't get out of there fast enough. For a brief moment, he thought about letting her go, but he couldn't bring himself to do so. Instead, he jogged the few yards to catch up with her, calling her name as he tapped her on the back.

She spun around, the terror in her eyes surprising him. "Callum!"

Did she think he was going to hurt her? He held up his hands. "I'm sorry, I didn't mean to frighten you."

She bit her lip, glanced from side to side as if checking their surroundings and then finally met his gaze. "You didn't."

Muffin jumped up at him and although Callum scratched the dog's neck, giving him the attention he craved, his gaze stayed on Chelsea. They stared at each other a few long moments and, finally, she broke the silence.

She nodded back toward the café. "Were you and Lachlan discussing the new restaurant?"

"Yep." But that's not what he wanted to discuss with her. "Chelsea, I…"

"Yes?" She prompted when he stalled.

Damn she was beautiful. Her cheeks were a rosy red—whether from the cool air or something else he couldn't tell but he'd never felt so tongue-tied in his life. "I just wanted to say I'm sorry about how I left things the other night."

She raised her eyebrows and reached up to tuck some flyaway hair behind her ear. "Why? We were both perfectly clear on what we were doing. You don't need to feel bad. I had a great day. And night."

"Well. Great. It's just…" He wasn't a one-night-stand kind of guy. They were only a few feet apart and he knew he couldn't walk away again. "I was wondering if you'd like to get together again sometime?"

Thank God no one but Chelsea could hear him. His brothers would never let him live it down if they heard him fumbling over asking a woman out.

Her tongue darted out to moisten her lips and then she rubbed them together. "You mean, like a date?"

What was the correct answer here? He didn't want to scare her off. "If that's what you'd like or we could just, you know, hang out."

"Hang out?" she echoed him as if she'd never heard of the concept before.

His pulse picked up. "Yes. That's if you want, but if you'd rather not."

"Oh, I want to," she admitted. The way she looked at him and the tone of her words indicated she understood that when he'd said "hang out" he'd imagined doing so without any clothes on. "I think hanging out is a good plan. When were you thinking?"

"Does right now sound too desperate?"

Her whole face lit up and sparkled as she laughed. "Right now sounds great, but, what about your brother?"

"Who?" For a second Callum forgot there was anyone else in the world except the two of them. "Oh, him. Right. We're pretty much done. He said yes to opening the restaurant, but he's a control freak and wants to do it all himself."

"That's great. I think."

"It is." He nodded. "I have plenty to keep me busy, and I know Lachlan will do a good job." But he didn't want to talk about Lachlan, the restaurant or the distillery. He didn't want to talk period. "Did you walk? Do you want me to give you a lift back to your place?"

She grinned and looked at him in a way that turned his insides liquid. "What about Lachlan?"

"What about him?" Callum asked as he closed the distance between them and gave in to the compulsion to kiss her.

Chapter Nine

It was official. Chelsea needed her head read. So much for one night, so much for not getting involved with Callum McKinnel. Fate be cursed for throwing them into each other's paths again. How the hell could she say no to that delicious face asking if she wanted to hang out with him? How could she keep any kind of clear head when he was kissing her like the world would end if he stopped?

Summoning all the willpower she had, she grabbed on to the single cell of common sense in her body and palmed her hands against his lovely, solid chest. "Someone might see us," she hissed, trying to summon some kind of care factor when all she could think about was kissing him again. And then some.

Callum pouted as he looked down at her. He was sexy when he smiled, but damn near irresistible when he scowled. "Ah right, your business reputation and all." His tone said he had little respect for what she did and while perhaps she *should* care about that, she didn't; what he thought of her career didn't matter. All that mattered right now was getting naked with him again, but doing so on the sidewalk would be unwise on a number of levels.

"Yes, my business," she whispered. "And the fact I don't want either of us to get arrested."

He chuckled at that, then took Muffin's lead from her hand and grabbed hold of it with his other hand. "I'd say your place or mine, but yours is closer."

Her hormones wouldn't have let her argue even if she wanted to. Which she didn't. She'd been jumpy and on edge these last few days—feeling someone was watching her—and when Callum had tapped her on the back, she'd almost jumped a mile. She welcomed the chance to take her mind off her paranoia for a couple of hours.

Callum all but dragged her to his parked SUV. As if they'd done this a hundred times before, he opened the passenger door for her and Muffin jumped in first. They laughed as the dog crossed over to the driver's seat and settled in for the ride. Chelsea climbed into the SUV and, as she clicked her seat belt into place, he closed the door and jogged around to his side. She dragged Muffin over to her long enough for Callum to climb into the car, but the moment he sat down, the dog scrambled onto his lap.

Once again, Callum navigated the short distance to her place with Muffin hindering his view. It was the funniest, yet most endearing, sight she'd ever seen.

The nosy old lady from next door was out front in

her garden when Callum parked in Chelsea's drive. Knowing what it felt like to be lonely, Chelsea often stopped to chat, but not today. Today she and Callum all but ran to the front door, trying not to trip over Muffin as he wound in and out of their legs, catching their excitement. On her porch, Callum took her key from her hand and unlocked the door—a little voice inside her considered objecting to this controlling action, but it could barely be heard over her screaming hormones. Sometimes scruples weren't worth the effort.

They stepped inside, and Callum had barely kicked the door shut before he spun her round and pressed her up against it. She felt his firm body mold against her as he smashed his mouth over hers. If she'd thought their previous kisses hot, they had nothing on this one. Ravaged, *beautifully ravaged*—these were the words that entered her head as he slipped his hands inside her coat and roved them all over her body. Her head fell back against the door as he slowly, tantalizingly rid her of her clothes until she was standing in her hallway naked and he was still fully clothed.

"You're freaking gorgeous," he said, his voice low as he looked and touched his fill. Shivers flooded her entire body, yet she was hotter than she'd ever been before.

"I was thinking the same about you," she whispered back, "but I do think you're slightly overdressed for the occasion."

"Am I? Sorry." Callum chuckled and gazed hungrily at her. "What do you suggest we do about that?"

In reply, she reached out and yanked his jacket off him, hurling it onto the pile of her own clothes at their feet. It looked and felt expensive, but she didn't care and he didn't seem to either. Next she stripped him of his shirt and pants, and her breath hitched as she stopped to admire him. Not sure if she'd ever be lucky enough to have him like this again, Chelsea took a moment to admire every chiseled muscle. His hands hung at his side as she reached out and ran her finger over his lips and then down his strong neck over his hard chest and even lower. His muscles tightened beneath her touch and when his erection flared large and proud, she had to bite her lower lip to stop from whimpering. She dropped to her knees, wanting to taste him and wanting to drive him crazy as he had done to her.

Callum groaned as she took him into her mouth and she glanced upward to see him palm his hands against the wall. She smiled around his penis, loving the taste and the feel of it in her mouth. It wasn't long before she felt him twitching inside her and then his hands were in her hair, yanking her back. He wasn't gentle but that only enhanced her arousal.

"Stop," he growled, "before it's too late."

"Too late for what?" she asked, looking up at him and smiling like the Cheshire Cat. Knowing what she could do to him was like a heady drug and she didn't *want* to give it up.

"This," he said, hauling her up and into his arms. He kissed her hard on the mouth as he lifted her up and dragged her legs around his waist. He slammed inside her and she cried out in surprised pleasure, loving the feel as he filled her completely. He was strong and had stamina and he took care of her, refusing to let go himself until she was a writhing, needy mess. And then he took it home, thrusting hard one final time and taking them both over the edge.

She clung to him, their skin hot and sweaty despite the temperature outside, as her heart rate slowly returned to normal. Or as close to normal as it could be with a naked Callum still in close proximity.

"Jeepers," he muttered after a few long minutes.

Chelsea laughed. "That's one word for it."

"Sorry," he said, "I got a little carried away. Next time I'll try to make it to your bedroom."

Sorry? Carried away? She had no complaints whatsoever. But, *next time?*

"Is that too presumptuous of me?" he asked as if he could read her mind.

She swallowed, unable to think straight with him still inside her. "Shall we take this conversation to the kitchen? Do you want a drink or something?"

"Sounds like a good idea." He gently eased her down his body and she thought again how strong he was to have been able to hold her like that for so long.

"Do you, uh…need to use the bathroom or anything?" She nodded toward his groin.

He grinned. "Do you? We could save water."

And man, it sounded like a line but she fell for it anyway.

Much later, once they were both dry, dressed and sitting on the bar stools at her kitchen counter sipping hot chocolate, she broached the issue of next time. "Did you mean it about seeing each other again?"

His lovely long fingers wrapped around her favorite mug—with a cocker spaniel that was almost Muffin's doppelganger painted on the front—he looked right into her eyes again. "Yes. I don't know what it is about you, Chelsea, but I've spent the last week trying not to think about you so I could focus on my work.

Problem is, trying not to think about you is almost as distracting as thinking about you."

Heat rushed to her cheeks and she pursed her lips together to stop the ridiculous smile that threatened to burst onto her face. It might not have been your standard sweet nothing—he'd almost made her sound an inconvenience—but no one else had ever said something that made her glow so much inside. She should run a mile in the opposite direction.

"So yes," he said, "I meant it about seeing you again. I'd like that very much. What do you say?"

Lord, it was tempting. But was it worth the risk? To her or his heart she wasn't sure, all she knew was that she didn't do relationships.

He raised his eyebrows as he gazed down at her. "It's not algebra, sweetheart. I'm simply asking if you want to hang out with me on a more regular basis?"

"Like a relationship?"

He nodded. "If you're asking if I'll be monogamous then a 100 percent yes, but I'll admit, I'm not looking to rush into marriage or anything."

"Well, good," she said, "because I'm warning you now, I'm not great with commitment. You should know that I'll probably get sick of the sight of you within a couple of months."

He laughed as if he found this notion hugely amusing. "Then, let's agree to take things one day at a time. What do you say?"

Oh shoot, what am I getting myself in for? "I guess I say, yes, but what about your family? What about my business? Do you think—"

Callum put his index finger against her mouth to silence her. "I think you're overthinking this. Let's just have fun together, okay?"

She sighed. "Okay." And then he smiled and kissed her again and she forgot why this wasn't such a good idea after all.

When they finally came up for air again, Callum gestured to the half-finished jigsaw puzzle on her small kitchen table. "You like puzzles?"

She remembered how she'd had one on the go the day her house was broken into and how he'd picked up the scattered pieces and put them back into the box.

"Yes. My granddad always had one on the go and I used to help him. It was our thing." She smiled nostalgically. "Stupid but it kinda makes me feel close to him even though he's gone." And it gave her something to do on long lonely nights when she thought she'd go insane if she had to watch any more crap television.

"That's not stupid," he said, pushing back his stool, then standing and walking the few steps to the table. He glanced down at the puzzle, then looked back over to her. "May I?"

"Please, go ahead."

Callum bent over the table and his brow furrowed as he studied the pieces. "Got one," he shrieked after a few moments.

Chelsea couldn't help but smile at his joyful expression.

She slid off her own stool and went over to join him, immediately finding a piece she'd been looking for. She pushed it in between four other pieces. "Bingo."

Callum grinned at her. "I reckon this could be addictive."

"It is. Trust me."

For a few minutes they sat in comfortable silence, shuffling through the puzzle pieces, congratulating each other and sharing the joy when one of them found a bit they could place. Finally, the dog she'd been working on for days started to take shape.

"This dog is a dead ringer for Muffin," he said.

She nodded. "I know. I couldn't resist it when I saw it. Just as I couldn't resist him."

"I'll bet he was cute as a pup."

"I wouldn't know; I got him from a shelter when he was a few years old, but I'm sure he was adorable. The hardest part was leaving all the other homeless animals behind."

"That was a charitable thing to do. Most people can't resist getting a puppy."

"Most people don't know what it's like to be passed from pillar to post all their lives. I do. I never want to feel like that again."

She didn't know why she was telling him this— it had taken her years to open up to Rosie and she'd never confessed her feelings to anyone else. "Anyway, I wanted to give a dog who really needed me a home."

Callum didn't say anything, but he reached out, took her hand and squeezed it. The simple gesture had tears pricking at the corner of her eyes, but she blinked them back, not wanting to cry like a big baby in front of him. After a few moments, he let go of her hand and looked at his watch. "I guess I'd better be heading back to the distillery."

He sounded as reluctant to go as she was to let him but she simply nodded, not wanting to appear needy in any way whatsoever.

As he pushed the stool back and stood, the phone on

the wall began to ring and Chelsea's heart leaped up into her throat at the thought it might be her frequent caller. She scrambled across the kitchen, yanking the cord out of the wall before her answering machine had the chance to request a message.

Callum raised an eyebrow and she summoned a carefree smile to her face. He was the kind of guy who would freak out if he heard her heavy breather, and she didn't want him to worry about her. The police didn't seem overly concerned, so why should she bother him with it.

"I've been getting all these sales calls lately. I'm over it," she said, and then to distract him she closed the distance between them and kissed him.

"Jeez," he said, running a hand over his beard when she pulled back, "if you kiss me again like that, I'm not going to be able to leave."

She shrugged apologetically. "And the problem with that is…?"

He shook his head and smiled. "*Vixen*. I really have to go before Sophie sends out a search party, but I won't be staying away for long. And that's a promise. Are you free tomorrow night?"

She was of course—her social calendar was as bare as a newborn's bottom—but she didn't tell him that. "How about Friday night?"

He nodded. "Okay. I'll pick you up, we can go out for dinner or something."

The speed at which this was going made her head spin. She felt the need to call a few shots. "How about I come to you this time? We can order pizza. I still feel like it's a bit early to be seen out in public with you. I know Bailey was the one to end your engagement, but…well, I don't feel like we should rub this in her face."

"Fair point. Scrap the pizza. I'll cook for you."

It was her turn to raise an eyebrow. "I thought Lachlan was the chef in your family?"

"I'll concede he's not bad, but wait till you see me in an apron!"

"Now that is something I can't wait for," Chelsea said as she and Muffin escorted Callum to the front door. There she kissed him goodbye, the both of them pulling back just as things threatened to get out of control again. She couldn't help grinning as she stood on the porch waving him off.

This feeling probably wouldn't last long but she was damn well going to make the most of it while it did. With that thought, she went inside and headed to her computer to answer inquiries for breakups.

Callum couldn't remember the last time he'd looked forward to something as much as cooking dinner for and hanging out with Chelsea on Friday night. Sophie had caught him honest-to-God whistling at work today, and even a grumpy old man he'd had to deal with on the tasting floor couldn't take the spring out of his step. It might only have been two days since he'd seen Chelsea, but that felt far too long.

Although his house was usually neat and tidy thanks to his cleaning guy, this afternoon he'd left the office early to cook dinner and make sure everything was perfect. He'd checked for any lingering evidence of Bailey and done a few more pieces of the puzzle he'd dug out of his mom's games cupboard yesterday. Okay, so having a puzzle on the go was perhaps a little try-hard but he wanted to make Chelsea feel comfortable in his space. So much so that when buying the ingredients for dinner, he'd even bought a big, juicy bone for Muffin. The way to a man's heart might be through his stomach but he reckoned the way to Chelsea's was through her dog. Luckily, he liked the mutt almost as much as he liked her.

Half an hour before she was due to arrive, with his lasagna in the oven and the garlic bread ready to go under the grill, he had a quick shower. He was toweling himself dry when the doorbell rang. He peeled back his bedroom curtain, which gave him a view of the grounds in front of his cottage, and he saw Chelsea's little car parked out front. Perhaps she was as eager as he to get this evening started.

About to pull on his boxers, Callum paused and thought again. Then, his grin still wide, he walked through to the kitchen, grabbed his apron off the hook, wrapped it around his waist and went to open the door.

Muffin burst inside before either of them could say anything to each other. Callum chuckled and called over his shoulder, "Make yourself at home, buddy." Then he turned all his attention on Chelsea. She was holding a small gift-wrapped box and was dressed from head to toe in warm weather-appropriate attire. The only flashes of skin he could see were her face and hands. He shivered as the winter breeze whooshed inside.

"You're early."

"I am." She smiled and glanced slowly down his body; his skin heated as if she'd touched him. "And you're wearing an apron."

"I warned you I would."

"You did. I just imagined you'd be wearing something else, as well."

"Do you have a problem with nudity?"

She shook her head. "Not yours."

"Good." And then he pulled her inside, kicked the door shut behind them, took the box from her hands, dropped it onto his hall table and pulled her into his arms. She tasted so good—if anything, even better than he remembered—and he wanted to devour her. If the hands that landed on his buttocks were anything to go by, Chelsea's thoughts were heading in the same illicit direction as his.

As much as he'd happily take her right there against the wall, he summoned some restraint.

"This is a nice place you've got," she muttered, glancing around as he took her hand and led her down the hallway. "It's got a lovely warm vibe to it."

"Thanks. It was my grandparents' place when we were growing up, but when my grandma died a few years ago, my granddad moved out. Too many memories or something." That was all the history he gave her before closing the bedroom door behind them and lifting his fingers to the buttons on her shirt.

Later, when they lay beneath his bed covers, arms and limbs still entwined, Chelsea's head resting on his shoulder, Callum tried to recall a moment in time when he'd felt like this before. There was just something about Chelsea that got under his skin, but he still wondered if it actually meant anything more than sex. After everything with Bailey, he no longer knew whether to trust his own feelings.

"Is something burning?" Her question interrupted his thoughts and he sat bolt upright.

"Shit. The lasagna."

Chelsea laughed as he shot out of bed and hurried to the kitchen. A few moments later as he stared into the oven at what *was* going to be their dinner, he felt like weeping. He'd slaved all afternoon over a hot stove to impress her and now all he had to offer was carcinogen poisoning.

"Dammit." Ignoring the smoke that wafted out of the oven, he grabbed a tea towel to stop from burning himself and lifted the disaster out onto the stove top.

Chelsea chose that moment to come up beside him. "Hmm…" was all she said.

"Sorry." He shook his head as he turned to look at her—she'd taken a moment to pull on the shirt that he had hanging over the end of the bed and she looked amazing in it.

"That'll teach you to open the door to me wearing nothing but an apron."

"At least I haven't killed the garlic bread. And I have cupcakes."

Her lips curled at the edges. "You made me cupcakes?"

And dammit, he wanted to say yes. "I… Okay, no, I bought them. There's a bakery in town and you haven't lived until you've tasted their cupcakes."

She laughed. "Garlic bread and cupcakes for dinner sounds good to me then. Truly, it's the company that matters and I'm quite enjoying yours."

"The feeling is entirely mutual."

They got dressed again for dinner, taking turns watching the garlic bread cook to avoid any further culinary disasters.

"I had set the dining room table for us to eat in

there," Callum said, when the garlic bread was nice and crunchy, "but it seems overkill for what is essentially toast."

Chelsea agreed so they took their dinner of cupcakes, garlic bread and soda into his living room and set the feast down on his coffee table. It felt all kinds of wrong not to offer a guest in his home an alcoholic drink but he knew her well enough already to know her answer and he didn't want her to feel any kind of uncomfortable.

"Where'd you get this?" Chelsea asked, eyeing the barely started puzzle that also sat on the coffee table.

"You inspired me the other day, so I came home and raided Mom's cupboards. Feel free to help. I'm not very good."

"Back in a moment." She stood and went into the hallway, returning as promised a few moments later with the box she'd brought when she arrived. "Here," she said, handing it to him.

He took the box and unwrapped it to find a jigsaw puzzle of a glass of whiskey. The image, which consisted mostly of clear glass and amber fluid, sat on an oaky grained table. It was simple but beautiful and would be very tricky to do.

"I love it," he said. "Thanks, but do ya reckon you could help me finish this one first?"

"I'd love to," she replied, settling in beside him.

For the next few hours, they sat together on his sofa, eating, finding pieces of the puzzle and talking about everything from favorite bands to the history of the McKinnel Distillery. For someone who abstained from drinking alcohol, Chelsea showed a great deal of interest in his family business. She listened eagerly as he explained how his father and his father's twin brother had come across from Scotland in their early twenties to travel the US.

"They both got lucky over here—Dad met Mom and on impulse Uncle Hamish bought a lottery ticket and won a bit of money. When Dad decided to move to America for Mom, Hamish came too and they used his winnings to buy the land we're on right now. Coming from the Scottish Highlands region, the boys had been surrounded by whiskey distilleries all their lives. Hamish worked at a local one, where he started as a grain flipper, but he'd always had the ambition to start his own. They were two young men with a dream and because Mom was the reason for the move to America, they decided to use some of her family history in the label. One of her ancestors was a bootlegger—it's his face on our label and our signature bottle is also named after him.

"Not long after they barreled their very first batch, Hamish was killed in a car accident and Dad threw his heart and soul into fulfilling their dreams on his own. Mom took up the trade, as well—she learned to live and breathe distilling, and when I was born, her parents moved into this cottage to help look after me. By that time Mom and Dad had built the main house with the last of Hamish's winnings."

"Such a sad story," Chelsea said, "but I bet Hamish would be very proud of what your parents achieved. From what I can gather, they've come a long way from those early days."

Callum nodded. "I wish I'd known him."

"What about your father's parents? Are they still alive? Do they still live in Scotland?"

"Yes. They're in a nursing home now but we take turns going across to visit them. All of us except Sophie, Annabel and Mac have done a stint living in Scotland and working in a distillery there that is owned by Dad and Hamish's mentor."

"It must be wonderful to have something that glues your family together like this. I can see why you love this place so much."

He could see the sadness in her eyes when she said this and it made him realize just how lucky he was. "Yes, it is. Do you not see any of your family now?"

She shook her head. "Mom was never in contact with her parents and Dad's mom died before I was born. I was never much more than a burden to anyone in my family, and I haven't seen nor heard from any of Dad's family since he died."

He was racking his head for what to say to that, but she spoke first, directing the conversation back to him. "Do you guys do tours here?"

He nodded. "Yep, Sophie and Blair take turns running them twice daily."

"I'd love to go on one."

"Seriously?" Considering her stance on alcohol, she couldn't have surprised him more if she'd said she'd love to swim naked in the Deschutes River in the middle of winter.

"Yep. I'm interested in what you do."

He grinned. "In that case, why wait for Sophie or Blair to show you through, when I can give you a private tour right now?"

Chapter Ten

Why Chelsea found herself so fascinated with the workings of the distillery she didn't understand. But she found herself hanging on Callum's every word as she followed him to the distillery for a private tour and he told her about its history.

They'd put on their winter coats and boots and decided to leave Muffin in the cottage, chewing on the bone Callum had given him earlier.

The distillery was only a short walk from his place and he held her hand the whole way as they trekked across the frosty grounds toward it. This place was magical at night. Someone had strung fairy lights across the trees and the garden was lit up with hundreds of little lights, as well.

"Who looks after the grounds?" she whispered to him, not wanting to alert his family as they passed his mom's place.

"Mom, actually. She's never happier than when she's in the garden, although some of the heavy work is getting a bit hard for her lately."

The farther away they got from the cottage, the stronger the smell that permeated the air here grew. The aroma of whiskey had always turned her off in the past, but she found herself warming to it. She guessed it was a little like those people who didn't drink coffee but adored the smell.

Only a hundred or so yards in front of the main house was the beautiful building she'd been in the first time she came here. Callum had explained that in addition to his office, the building also held the tasting room, shop floor and small café. Off to one side of this building was a large barn-type structure.

"This is the actual distillery," he said, as they approached and he shone his flashlight at the massive oak entrance doors. "And behind the distillery is our storage and bottling facility. Not all distilleries bottle their own whiskey but it's something we pride ourselves on here at McKinnel's. As you know, I'd like to go one step further and farm our own grain, as well, but I might be getting a little ahead of myself."

If anyone could do it, Callum could, she thought as he took a big ring of keys out of his pocket and dropped her hand in order to open the door. Darkness engulfed them when the door swung back, but he flicked a switch that flooded the building with bright lights. In here the smell of alcohol was so strong, she screwed up her nose, thinking she might get drunk on the fumes.

Callum laughed. "You get used to the smell after a while. I must admit I barely notice it now." Now that there was light, he went over and closed the big doors behind them. "Temperature is very important when it comes to distilling, so we don't want to let the cold air inside."

She visibly shivered at his words and he laughed. "Right, let's get this tour started before we both freeze to death."

"Sounds good." She half laughed, but it didn't quite come out that way as nerves threatened to swallow her whole. The smell of whiskey was so potent, it brought back memories of her father and the rages he used to go into when he'd been on a bender. Which was pretty much every night.

"Are you okay?" Callum asked, a frown creasing his brow.

She nodded and lied. "Just cold. Tour away."

Still looking a little hesitant, Callum gestured for her to follow him and they crossed to the far end of the building. He cleared his throat. "Now, I warn you, I can get carried away when talking about this stuff, so feel free to interrupt or tell me to shut up."

She smirked. "Just get on with it, will you?"

"Yes, miss." He rewarded her with one of his tantalizing smiles and she made the decision to focus on that, on *him*, rather than where they were. "Okay, first thing is the grain and this is where we store it." He pointed to some large silver tanks. "All whiskey is made from some kind of grain—wheat, corn, rye, barley or a blend of these are the traditional ones, but anything goes these days. And lots of boutique distillers are trying other cereal grains."

"Would you ever consider doing so?" she asked.

He nodded. "It's one of the many ideas in my five-year plan, but Dad was dead set against it, so I need to tread carefully as I try to win the others round to the idea."

"Why is the type of grain so important?"

He smiled at her question. "The grain and how we treat it is the first step in determining the flavor of the finished product."

"I see."

"All you need to make whiskey is grain, yeast and water, but that doesn't mean it's easy to do."

Chelsea glanced around them at the rows of tanks, barrels and other large machinery she had no idea of. She could quite believe it.

Over the next little while, Callum walked her around the building, explaining each step of the distilling process in layman's terms so she could understand but also with the kind of passion that made her want him to speak forever.

He taught her about milling and mashing, fermentable sugars, brewing and the two types of stills used.

"Essentially whiskey is just distilled beer. First you make the beer from the grain, water and yeast, then the beer goes into the still for boiling. The alcohol and some flavor evaporate, leaving the water behind. Dad always used to say that beer is for impatient people who don't want to wait for moonshine, and moonshine is for impatient people who can't wait for whiskey."

He'd already mentioned that moonshine—baby whiskey—was what went into the barrel, and whiskey (or bourbon or Scotch, depending on where it was made and what grains were used) was what came out.

"Does it take a long time to make whiskey then?" she asked.

"Whiskey isn't genuine until it has been aged for a minimum of two years, so yes, it takes a while."

"Wow, I don't think my family ever appreciated the effort that went into making it when they were drinking it."

"Well, to be honest, as a distiller, I wouldn't want people to take as long to drink it as we do to make it, or we'd go out of business, but it's nice when connoisseurs take the time to do a tour and learn what they can."

They continued on to the area where the barrels were stored, each one stamped on the end with the McKinnel logo and the date the batch was barreled. The room felt a lot warmer than the rest of the building and was positively temperate compared to outside. "And did I mention all these barrels must be new American oak? That's the law—you can't call it a bourbon unless it's aged in new oak."

Callum's smile dazzled her as he spoke and every word that came from his mouth was so full of fervor that she couldn't help grinning.

He caught her looking and frowned. "What's so funny?"

She shook her head. "Not funny. Wonderful. You really love this stuff, don't you?"

He shrugged a shoulder. "Yeah. I guess I do. I've been feeling a bit jaded lately, but sharing it with you reminds me this is who I am. This distillery, it's in my blood. Without it, I wouldn't know what to do."

"Can I taste some?" The question surprised her almost as much as it did him.

His eyes widened. "What? You serious? I don't want you to feel pressured just because we're here. I wouldn't want to make you do anything you don't feel comfortable with."

She swallowed. If someone had told her a few weeks ago that she'd be voluntarily tasting whiskey, she'd have laughed in their face. But Callum made her want to push boundaries, to step outside her safety zone.

"You're not," she said. "I don't feel pressured at all. Watching you, and seeing your family at Thanksgiving, has shown me that alcohol isn't black and white. I don't want it to scare me anymore. Does that make any sense?"

"Yes, it does." He stepped closer and took her hand; his hand was warm despite the frosty temperatures. "Come on, let's go over to the tasting room."

As they left the actual distillery, Callum let go of Chelsea's hand only long enough to lock the door again, then he led her across to the building she'd gone into that first day they'd met. She'd been nervous the first time she stepped inside, but her heart beat wilder now than it ever had before.

What the heck was she getting herself into?

"Take a seat at the counter," Callum instructed. "Are you warm enough? Do you want me to get the fire going? There's something about tasting whiskey with a roaring fire in the background, I always think."

"That would be great," she said, more to delay the tasting than anything else. As she looked around this gorgeous building—brimming with McKinnel family history—she fought to control the urge to turn and run away.

Callum shrugged off his coat and threw it across the black leather sofa by the fireplace. Chelsea watched, inhaling and exhaling deeply as he brought the fire to life. Pity she was far too apprehensive to appreciate the lovely view of his tight behind as he squatted low. When he was done, he straightened again, wiped his hands on his jeans and then crossed over to where she was perched on a stool. Smiling at her, he went behind the tasting counter, retrieved two funny-shaped glasses—like a bowl at the bottom but narrower at the top.

"Nosing or snifter glasses," he said. "These are for tasting whiskey, not generally for drinking it—the narrow rim helps channel and concentrate the aromas toward your nostrils, if you know what I mean."

She nodded and only just managed to reply, "I think so."

"Take your coat off, you should be relaxed when tasking whiskey."

Chelsea raised her eyebrows. Relaxed might be asking a little much, but she slipped off her coat and draped it over the stool beside her anyway.

Next Callum took a couple of bottles off the shelf on the back wall. "Remember how I said we have a few different varieties. I'll start you on our signature line—this is a bourbon, which means…"

"It's mostly corn," she interrupted, "and aged in charred new-oak barrels."

"I'm impressed." As he spoke, Callum poured a small amount into both glasses, then lifted one, swirled the liquid around inside and then handed it to her. "One of the first rules of drinking whiskey—or any alcoholic beverage for that matter—is that you must never do so alone. Drinking is a social thing. Or it should be."

Her stomach flipped as their fingers brushed, but she wasn't sure if it was his touch or the fact she was about to do something she'd always sworn she never would. He noticed her fingers shaking and reached out to steady her hand, wrapping his around hers and the glass as he looked right into her eyes. "Chelsea, you don't have to do this if you don't want to."

"I *do*." She wanted to *and* she needed to. Tasting Callum's whiskey would be like flipping her past the bird. Proving that no matter what happened between them, she would no longer let her past have such a strong hold on her.

"Okay, then," he whispered, easing his hand away from hers. "Take it slow. First look at the color—this will vary depending on the oak of the cask and how long the whiskey has been aging. Then stick your nose in the glass and have a smell. Then do it again and again. A whiskey's nose tells you a lot. If the smell intoxicates you, you're more likely to enjoy the drink."

She did as he said, aware of his eyes fixed on her. Not a sound could be heard except the crackling of the fire behind them. "I can actually smell caramel," she said after a few long moments.

A proud grin spread across Callum's face. "Not many amateurs smell anything the first time. You obviously have a nose for this."

Her stomach flipped at his compliment, giving her the courage to lift the glass to her mouth. "Okay. Here goes nothing." She sucked in a deep breath and then took a sip. As the liquid hit her tongue, it burned and she screwed up her whole face, spluttering as she swallowed.

"Yuck." She wiped her mouth with the back of her hand as if that would eradicate the aftertaste. "That's *ghastly*! It doesn't *taste* like caramel. How can anyone ever get addicted to *that*?"

Callum had never in his whole life seen anything quite as delightful as Chelsea's reaction to the whiskey. Her beautiful grimace would be imprinted on his mind forever.

"You know not all people who drink alcohol become alcoholics," he said, stretching out his hand and wrapping it around hers, "but I'm sorry that's mostly been your experience."

She shook her head. "Please, don't apologize. My past isn't your fault, but you're showing me the other side of the coin and for that I thank you." And then she lifted the nosing glass and took another sip.

Again, that grimace. This time, he couldn't help laughing.

"Does it get any better?" she asked, a smile blossoming on her face.

"Bourbon can be an acquired taste," he admitted, scrubbing his hand over his beard.

"I'm sorry." She rubbed her lovely lips together. "I'm being rude. This is the produce of your family's love and hard labor. I wonder if I'd like it better with soda or ice? Or is that a big no-no?"

He swallowed, almost losing focus on what she was saying because he was staring at her lips. "There are no rules. Some folks say you shouldn't drink whiskey anything but straight, some say even adding ice is sin, but I say—and this is one thing my father and I agreed on—that there is no one way to drink whiskey. Saying that, I don't want to force you. We can stop now if you like."

After all, he could think of many other ways to pass their time together.

"No." She shook her head and held out her glass. "Hit me with the next one."

He took the glass and put it to one side. "New whiskey, new glass. This one is our single malt, made with 100 percent malted barley," he explained as he poured her a measure. "It's basically a Scotch, but you can't call it that if it's made outside of Scotland. It'll taste quite different to the bourbon."

Chelsea took the glass, swirled the liquid and then lifted it to her mouth as if she'd been born tasting whiskey. "I can definitely taste the grain in this one," she said after taking a sip. "It's a lot more…"

"Malty?" he suggested.

"Yes," she shrieked. "That's it."

They both laughed.

"Do you like it any better?"

"No, I'm sorry but I don't. Although I never thought I could have this much fun tasting alcohol, the good news is, that after doing so, I think it's safe to say I'll never become an alcoholic. No offence but I much prefer hot chocolate or coffee."

"No offense taken." He wasn't sure any words that escaped *that* mouth could ever be offensive. "Now, shall we go back to my place and do the jigsaw puzzle?"

She raised an eyebrow and leaned a little across the counter toward him. "Is *jigsaw puzzle* code for something else, Callum?"

Heat flooded his body at the suggestiveness in her tone. "Do you want it to be?"

In reply, she leaned even farther forward and pressed her lips against his. This time when they kissed, he tasted McKinnel's own sweet whiskey on her tongue and the combination of Chelsea and the liquor he threw his heart and soul into turned him on like nothing ever had before. Taking her home would take too long. She didn't seem to have any complaints when he all but hauled her over to the rug in front of the still-burning fire and pulled her down onto the ground beside him.

"Oh, *Callum*," she whispered over and over again as he slowly undressed and seduced her. His name had never sounded so sweet as it did on her lips, no woman had ever tasted so good and he couldn't recall ever feeling as alive as he did when he was inside of her. It felt as if he'd known her forever, but a quick calculation revealed they'd barely been acquainted two weeks.

"I hope you don't have security cameras," Chelsea said, still resting her head on his chest and distracting him from his thoughts.

His arms tightened around her. "Shit. We do." He'd been so desperate to have her, he hadn't given a thought to such things.

"Oh no," she squealed, sitting upright and scrambling around them for her clothes.

As much as he enjoyed the view, he chose to put her out of her misery. "Relax, sweetheart, I'm the one who checks the cameras."

She paused in her frantic efforts and turned back to look at him, relief flooding over her face. "Can we go look now?"

He pretended to misunderstand. "You want to watch us in action? I didn't peg you for the kinky type."

Chelsea swatted him with her bra and glared. "I. *Meant*. To. Delete. It."

"I don't know." He shrugged. "That seems a bit of a shame, don't you reckon?" Although he was stringing her along, there was no way he'd ever leave evidence of this night lying around for his family to find. It was hard enough getting them to take him seriously as boss without a sex tape doing the rounds.

"Show me where the recordings are. Now!" Chelsea demanded, standing and dressing quickly. "Or I'll… I'll…"

He laughed and pulled her back into his arms. "Relax. We'll delete them right away."

They took longer to get dressed than they had to get naked, possibly because Callum kept getting distracted. Then, like a couple of naughty teenagers, they headed down the hallway and snuck into his office to erase all evidence of their sordid shenanigans.

Chapter Eleven

After wolfing down a bowl of Froot Loops, Chelsea opened her door and stepped onto her front porch right into a pile of... She looked down and screwed up her nose in shocked disgust.

Is that horse manure?

Trying not to vomit, she lifted her foot out of the mess and shouted at Muffin, who had all but buried his nose in the pile, to get back. She shoved him inside, closed the door behind her and yanked off both her boots, which were going immediately into the trash. Then she stepped around the poo and peered left and right, trying to see if there were any signs of whoever had left it there.

Nope. Nothing. Not even a car on the road. It was almost eerily quiet out the front of her house. Maybe she should be scared, but right now Chelsea was too furious about her favorite pair of boots to be anxious. She yanked her cell phone out of her purse and almost gagged as she snapped a few shots of her morning delivery, the pungent smell wafting upward as she did so. Knowing she'd need to clean it up before she went out, which would likely make her late for today's job, she went back inside first, shutting the door and then double-checking that she'd locked it. Muffin looked up at her with big wide eyes as if wondering what he'd done to make her punish him.

"I'm sorry, sweet pea, but I think our heavy breather has struck again." As she admitted her fears out loud, her heart raced a little faster. The last couple of weeks she'd spent a fair few nights at Callum's house. The nights she didn't, he often came to her place. However she'd had an early appointment today and Callum an important meeting, so last night they'd only spoken on the phone. Exhausted from night after night of little sleep, she'd slept like a baby, but the idea that while she'd been slumbering some creep had been lurking around outside her house, leaving presents, took the edge off that sleep. It brought back the fears she'd been trying to swallow since the phone calls had started— the fear that someone was watching her every move.

Not wanting to feel like she couldn't sleep soundly in her own home, Chelsea called up Officer Fernandez, hoping he'd take this latest thing more seriously than he had her reports of threatening calls.

He answered after a few rings.

"Hi, Officer, it's Chelsea Porter here." She paused a moment, giving him the chance to place her.

"Hello, Chelsea. Have you had any more calls? Has the caller identified themselves or made any actual threats yet?" he asked, his tone a little condescending, as if he really didn't have time for this and would much rather deal with something more exciting. Perhaps a murder? Should she try to speak to someone else? Demand Sergeant Moore get back on her case? At least he'd been kind and seemed to take it seriously when Muffin had disappeared.

"I disconnected my home phone, so haven't had any more calls—" Thankfully whoever was behind all this hadn't gotten hold of her cell number yet. "But this morning I got a delivery and I'm sure it's linked to the heavy breather."

"What was this delivery?" He sounded marginally interested.

"A big, smelly pile of horse poo."

This announcement was met with a few moments' silence and then the moron exploded into laugher.

Chelsea raised her eyebrows and her grip tightened on the phone. "I fail to see the amusing side of this, Officer. How would you like it if I delivered said pile of manure to your desk?"

He cleared his throat. "I'm sorry. Quite right."

"I've taken some photos I can send through to you if you like."

"Send away." He chuckled again. "Nothing I like better than a few good photos of shit to start my day."

Chelsea's jaw clenched. "Are you actually going to do anything about this?"

"Of course. I'll come over today and knock on some doors, ask the neighbors if they saw anyone suspicious and then you can let me know if any of the descriptions sound anything like any of the people you've previously done *business* with." Again, he couldn't hide his amusement when speaking about her work, but at least he'd agreed to investigate this time. Still, she was tired of people not taking her work seriously.

"I've got to go out now to…do some *business*… but I'll be back in half an hour or so. Shall I leave the evidence on the porch or will the photos be enough?"

"I'm sure one pile of horse manure is much the same as another," Fernandez said. "I'll make do with the photos."

"Okay." She uttered reluctant thanks, then said, "I'll send them through in a moment."

"Great. Have a good morning, Ms. Porter. I'll be in touch."

Having no confidence whatsoever that Fernandez would even look at the photos, she emailed them to him and then set about removing the evidence and disinfecting the entire length of her front porch. Perhaps she should take comfort from the fact the cops didn't seem overly concerned about her problem. As she hosed down the porch, she decided that if whoever was doing this was a real threat, surely they would have done something more drastic by now.

Chelsea finished the cleanup, then went inside, showered and changed into a whole new outfit. She glanced at her watch, hoping today's dumpee was still at the gym—according to Garth's soon-to-be ex-girlfriend, he was a weight-lifting junkie and, without fail, went every morning. She was glad she'd arranged today's meeting for a public place—she didn't always insist on this, but what with the burglary, the phone calls and now the poo, she didn't want to be alone in private with anyone she didn't know.

After the short drive into town, she parked in front

of the gym, then checked his photo and the details of the breakup on her phone, before getting out. She left Muffin in the front seat of the car with the window down for air and went over to wait outside the entrance. Somehow she'd made it here five minutes before Garth's girlfriend had predicted he would leave.

Exactly five minutes later, the door to the gym opened and out strode one of the bulkiest guys Chelsea had ever seen. While he had a classically handsome face, she had to try hard not to grimace at the sweaty, bulgy muscles that weren't hidden at all beneath his sweatpants and sweatshirt. Bulky dudes just weren't her cup of tea. Tall and lean like Callum—that was how she liked them.

Garth saw her looking and smiled warmly. "Hey," he said as he continued on his way.

Chelsea bit her lip and hung back, almost paralyzed. Although Garth seemed like a friendly bloke, she had a vision of exactly what he could do if he wanted to hurt her. But unease wasn't the only thing holding her back. The last week or so, for the first time since she'd started her business, she'd found herself beginning to dread the face-to-face meetings where she had to deliver the bad news to someone's boyfriend or girlfriend. It was hard to be stoic about ending a relationship when she herself was living in a bubble of bliss.

Because that was the only definition for what she had going on with Callum. Granted it was early days—generally she didn't feel the need to detach herself from someone until the two- or three-month mark—but this thing with him felt different already. The shine of her new relationship hadn't even begun to wear off. Her attraction toward him was strong, if not stronger, than that first moment she'd laid eyes on him. But it was no longer simple chemistry that drew her to him, it was much more—they had fun together. She didn't even care that he made his money from making whiskey—and this scared the hell out of her.

For the first time, Chelsea found herself thinking of a future with a man. For the first time, she felt the risk of getting hurt.

Callum and her relationship was still a national secret, due mostly to her fears that her professional reputation would be sacrificed if it got out that they were seeing each other. Of course that wouldn't be a problem if she stopped doing this and did something else instead. But what would she do? She'd enjoyed waitressing but she wasn't passionate enough about it to want to make a career out of it. And, although Callum undoubtedly savored her company, he'd not given any indication of wanting anything more serious. Since Thanksgiving, he'd made no suggestions she meet his family again nor mentioned anything more than red-hot fun.

Muffin barked as Garth passed Chelsea's car on his way to hers and the sound jolted her back to the present. No matter if she was questioning her career, she had an obligation to follow through on all current jobs and Garth was one of them. Spurred into action, she called out his name as she started jogging toward him.

As they didn't have a private room big enough to accommodate the whole family in the distillery buildings, Sophie had called the family meeting at their mom's dining table. It had taken almost a month to find a time when everyone could attend, and Callum was biting at the bit to get started. Unfortunately, the rest of his family didn't appear to share his urgency and right now only his mom and Sophie were here.

"I'll go gather the troops," Sophie said, pushing back from her seat at the table and hurrying out.

Callum tapped his fingers on the dining room table.

"Relax," his mom said from across the table. She poured him a glass of orange juice and then pushed it toward him. "They'll be here soon. How's that lovely girl you brought to Thanksgiving? Is it her car I've been seeing parked outside your cottage late some nights? I can't help but notice on the nights her car isn't there, your SUV is often absent also."

He took a sip of juice and leveled his eyes with hers. "You ever considered a job with the FBI?"

She laughed. "I only notice what matters to me, and you, my darling, matter. While I'm sorry to see you and Bailey go your separate ways, Chelsea seemed lovely. If things are getting serious in that department, maybe you should bring her over for dinner again soon?"

Callum spluttered. "Serious? Who said anything about serious, Mom? I know you're desperate for more grandbabies but my focus right now is the distillery. You know that." He'd meant it when he said he didn't have time for a relationship—he'd barely seen Bailey the last few weeks they'd been together—but he was making time for Chelsea and enjoying every moment of it. Nora opened her mouth to say something more and Callum prepared himself for a lecture on the balance of work and play, but the dining room door swung open again and Sophie returned, all her siblings bar one in tow.

"I called Mac," she said, taking her seat at the table

again. "He's only a few minutes away." Mac had a massive, architecturally designed house on one side of the formation in the mountains that gave Jewell Rock its name—from his front porch, he overlooked the whole town—but until recently he'd barely lived there.

"Good," Callum grunted and took another sip of orange juice as he checked the PowerPoint presentation for the umpteenth time.

While his siblings helped themselves to drinks and Nora encouraged them all to devour the feast she'd laid out on the table, Callum glanced over at the photo of his dad on the mantel.

I promise I'm doing all this for the greater good, he said silently, knowing that if Conall McKinnel were still alive, none of what he was about to propose would stand a chance.

"How's Hamish doing? I haven't seen him since Thanksgiving," Annabel said to Lachlan before shoving a piece of Mom's chocolate brownie into her mouth. Hanging around all the guys at the firehouse had taken the edge off her femininity, but he'd heard she had plenty of admirers so it didn't seem to be doing her any harm.

"He's great." That proud grin Lachlan got whenever he talked about his son came onto his face. "He's just joined the school chess club, so we're living and breathing it at home at the moment."

Annabel smiled. "I'll have to give him a game. But you'll have to warn him, I'm pretty good—we often play it while waiting at work."

Listening, Callum bit back a smile. For some reason the idea of all these big, burly firefighters sitting around playing chess caused him amusement.

At that moment, Mac entered the room—looking as grumpy as he had every day since quitting the team. "Sorry I'm late," he muttered, as he sat down beside Blair and surveyed the table. "Have we got anything else aside from OJ?"

"I can get you some water if you'd like, Owen," Mom said, and although she sounded perfectly warm, the fact she'd used his proper name let everyone know it was a reprimand. Nothing escaped Mom's notice and, like Callum, she'd observed that Mac had been drinking a fair amount of late.

"Let's get started," Callum said, clearing his throat. He looked to Sophie sitting beside him and she nodded, pushed a few buttons on his laptop and the first slide of their presentation appeared on the wall behind them. "Thank you all for coming today. With Sophie's help, I want to show you a few ideas I have for the business. We've divided these into four main areas and created a five-year plan, showing how we would like to roll them out. Area one is merchandise, which will be Sophie's baby, so I'll let her talk about that more in a moment. Area two is entertainment and hospitality. You know I want to expand the café into a restaurant and I'm pleased to announce that Lachlan is willing to come on board as head chef. The restaurant, how it runs, its style, et cetera, will all be his vision, but," he turned to look at Mac, "the café area we currently have is too small, so we'll need someone to oversee the building of an extension. Mac, I'd love you to head this project if you have the time."

Mac's eyes widened and then he blinked as if he wasn't sure whether to be offended or appreciative of the offer.

"No need to give me a definitive answer right now," Callum said, "I'd just like you to think about it. And if you're interested, then Lachlan, you and I can talk more later."

Quinn piped up. "You make this all sound like a done deal. Is there any point the rest of us being here?"

"Quinn," Nora chastised, "stop being a spoiled brat and listen to your brother's ideas."

Callum tossed his mom a grateful smile. "Also in the area of entertainment and hospitality is the option of holding events such as weddings and other celebrations on our grounds. We've got plenty of space for a marquee in the summer months and with the new restaurant, we'll be able to offer catering, as well." He didn't mention that this idea had been Chelsea's, but her face came into his head and he couldn't help smiling at the thought of her.

"This all sounds fabulous," Annabel said, reaching for another brownie. "I'm almost a little sad I don't work here."

"You just say the word and we'll find a job for you."

Annabel grinned. "I'll give it serious thought." But they all knew she'd never leave the firehouse.

"Area three is distilling." Callum continued quickly before Quinn could make a snide remark about their whole business being distilling. "I've been talking to Blair about the possibility of expanding our range— maybe starting to sell white dog, marketing it as a good replacement for vodka in cocktails. In the restaurant, we can have a range of cocktails and even the odd demonstration about how to make them. There's also the option of experimenting with more grains and..."

"White dog?" Quinn scoffed. "Dad would never

have gone for that. In fact, he'd have hated all of this. He hated change."

Callum clenched his fists. "And that was fine twenty, thirty or forty years ago when we were the only one of our kind around, but you'd have to be blind not to have noticed all the other boutique distilleries popping up in the region. We're not only competing with the big-brand bourbons now, we're up against the beer, rum and vodka guys to name a few in our own backyard. If we don't start to make a few changes, we'll go under. Is that what you want?"

Quinn glowered back, his cheeks flushing red. Callum realized he was practically shouting and he glanced apologetically at his mom, but she smiled encouragingly and spoke for the first time since the meeting had officially started.

"No one wants that, Callum, and I have to say I'm liking all these ideas. Go on, please."

He took a quick breath and then hit them with area four. "Grain production. Now hear me out," he said, when a few of his siblings made noises of surprise. "I've been looking at the farming land adjacent to ours and am in discussions with the owner, who is wanting to ease into retirement. If we lease some of his land and grow our own grain, in the long term, we'll save a huge amount of money and have more control over the quality of the grain we use."

"I love the idea," Blair said, "but, just one question— who is going to farm this grain of ours? Aside from Mom, none of us is exactly a green thumb."

Callum looked across to his sister and winked. "Annabel?"

When the laughter had died down, he took heart

that, except for Quinn, everyone seemed enthusiastic about his ideas. "We'll hire a farm manager of course."

Quinn, although sounding more resigned, had one final bugbear. "All this sounds mighty expensive."

Callum opened his mouth to reply but Mom got there first. "What's that saying about having to spend money to make money?"

Her enthusiasm surprised him; he'd thought she'd be more reluctant, hold on to the distillery as her husband and his brother had envisioned, but if anything, she sounded as excited as him.

Quinn held his hands up in surrender. "Alright, you've almost convinced me, but can I make one suggestion?"

"Anything," Callum said, thrilled that it had been a lot easier to win Quinn around than he'd thought.

"These events you want to run? Do you think we could outsource the planning to Bailey? She's hoping to quit working in Bend to start her own events-management company."

"Really?" It was the first Callum had heard of it, and he couldn't help but wonder why Quinn knew so much about Bailey. Then again, they'd been in the same year at school and still had a number of mutual friends, so that probably accounted for it. Whatever, he didn't have the time or inclination to think about this any further.

"Sure," he said, "if everyone else is agreeable."

His family nodded in unison. Working with Bailey could be a good thing—they could reestablish a professional friendship—and if not, well, she'd mostly be dealing with Lachlan and Sophie he imagined.

"Just one more thing, I also had this idea about how

we could promote responsible drinking among our customers and patrons of the restaurant."

Quinn, back on form, scoffed, "You want to encourage our customers *not* to drink?"

"No." He shook his head, annoyed. But the thought of Chelsea and her background made him continue. While he wasn't about to take responsibility for all the alcoholics on the planet, being with her had reminded him of the vulnerability some people had where alcohol was concerned. "But being seen to be aware of alcohol abuse could be good for business. I was thinking about partnering up with the local taxi company to offer a discount for restaurant diners, or maybe even offering a free dinner to the driver."

"Another innovative idea, big brother," Annabel said. "I'm in favor of anything that might reduce the number of motor vehicle accidents we have to attend."

"Thanks. But right now, it's just a thought. I know this has been a lot to take in at once, but does anyone have anything they want clarified?"

It was a stupid question. His mom, brothers and Annabel all opened their mouths and spoke at once. Even Mac seemed to show more enthusiasm for the future of the distillery than he had for anything in quite a while. Callum and Sophie spent the next hour or so answering questions and explaining various things in greater detail.

Then came the vote.

They'd always been an open family, so there was no secret ballot. However, the rules of the distillery were that every member of the family must be agreeable before anything new could go ahead.

Nora took on her role as matriarch. "All in favor of

going forward with the five-year plan presented today, raise your hand."

Callum held his breath, glancing around the table from face to face as one by one hands shot into the air. As he suspected, Quinn was the only one to hesitate, but just when Callum thought all was lost, a slow smile crept onto his younger brother's face and he raised his hand.

"Okay. Let's do this," Quinn said, and happy cheers burst all around them.

Callum pulled Sophie into a tight hug and whispered his thanks for everything into her hair. There were exciting times ahead for the McKinnels…he could feel it in his blood.

Chapter Twelve

"How was your day?" Callum asked after greeting her with a smoking-hot kiss. The way his green eyes glowed and the smile that stretched almost from ear to ear told her his day had been a great success and she couldn't wait to hear about it.

Her *day* flashed before her eyes in a series of snapshots—there was so much to tell him, but something held her back from including the whole horse manure thing. Not wanting to alarm him or make him feel obliged to protect her, she still hadn't mentioned the phone calls or the fact she felt like she was being followed, so this latest installment would come out of the blue.

"Okay." She sighed, still feeling a little heavy in her heart. While she was eternally single, her work had felt important, as if she was doing a service to others like herself who were unlucky in love, but now she wasn't so sure whether she *was* single or how she felt about her work. "I dumped a guy..."

"And?" he prompted, leading her into the house and down the hallway into the living room. Muffin had already collapsed on the rug in front of the fire.

"*And* it's hard to explain, but I didn't get the same satisfaction I usually do."

He frowned.

"*Satisfaction* isn't the right word," she said, frustrated that she couldn't explain herself well. "But when I'm spending time with someone after I've broken the bad news to them, I usually feel that it is time well spent. That I'm somehow helping them get through a tough time and that, by listening and talking to them, I'm giving them hope for a future. Today, when I told this poor guy, he was fighting back tears, and I felt like... I don't know...a tax collector or something."

Callum chuckled and pulled her down onto the couch with him. He caught her face in his two big palms and smiled down at her. "You do have an unusual career, but if it's not making you happy, maybe you should think about doing something else."

She blew air out between her teeth and felt her bangs fly up a little. She felt more unsettled than she had since those days when she'd had no real place to call home.

"But what would I do?"

Chelsea wasn't exactly expecting him to have an answer, but he surprised her by offering one. His expression turned serious and his tone matched. "Remind me again why your friend suggested you start a business of breaking up for people?"

"Because I have personal expertise in dumping men."

He half smiled. "I meant the other reason. Wasn't it because you were a good listener?"

She rubbed her lips together and nodded. "Yes. That too."

"I've certainly found that to be true," he said. "You've listened to me ramble on and on about the distillery for hours and always acted interested."

"That's because I am interested."

"Even though you come from a long line of alcoholics?"

And she nodded, realizing the terrifying fact that Callum could be talking about toilet paper designs and she'd still hang on his every word. How many nights over the last few weeks had they stayed up until the early hours of the morning talking? It was no longer just his body she craved when they were apart, but every single thing about him. The way he bit his lower lip and his brow creased when he was concentrating over a puzzle, his devotion to Muffin, his love for his family, his ambition, the way he looked in an apron— she could go on and on.

"You are an excellent listener," he said, and she took a moment to remember what they were talking about. "That gives you a fair few other career options."

"Oh?" Chelsea tried to focus on what he was saying when inside her heart was threatening cardiac arrest having just been told by her brain that she'd fallen in love. *Really?* She could hardly believe this alien concept, but it was the only explanation for the way she felt about Callum. The only reason the shine hadn't even begun to wear off their fling.

He counted off the possibilities on his fingers. "You

could become a hairdresser or you could host your own talk-radio show."

She felt her lips lift at the edges. "Are you simply plucking random careers from nowhere?"

He shook his head. "No, these are jobs where you're required to be a good listener. Or you could become a counselor and really make a difference with your wonderful talent for listening and knowing the right things to say to make people feel better."

"A counselor?" She tried the words on for size. "That would involve going to college or something."

"Which you'd excel at, I'm sure." Callum gave her an encouraging smile that not only melted her insides but boosted her confidence. He sounded like he actually believed in her. Aside from Rosie and her grandfather, when he wasn't blind drunk, no one else ever had.

"Hmm… You know, I would love to work with kids and teens who come from similar backgrounds to my own. Maybe you're on to something."

"Of course I am." He pulled her into his arms and kissed her, which resulted in all sensible thought vanishing from her head. She could barely think straight, never mind seriously plan her future when Callum's lips and hands were bestowing such attention upon her.

As was the way whenever she came to his place or he to hers, conversation waned for a while as other things, *wonderful, earth-shattering* things, took over. She let the physical sensations wash through her and tried to forget about the disquieting emotional ones.

After thoroughly ravishing each other, they turned their attentions to food. Callum outdid himself this time, managing to throw together a satay beef and noodle stir-fry without burning any of it. While they ate, she finally remembered to ask him about *his* day.

"Hey, how was your family meeting?" she asked between mouthfuls.

"Magic." He grinned, sounding like an excited schoolboy as he told her all about it.

"Everyone was really open to the new ideas. I feel awful admitting this, but it was such a different vibe to those meetings when Dad was at the head of the table, pooh-poohing anyone else's suggestions. I think I could have been sixty-five and he still wouldn't have given me any real responsibility; I just wish he didn't have to die to give me the chance."

"I guess it was hard for him to relinquish control of the company he and his brother had put their everything into. Maybe handing over any part of the business would have felt like losing even more of his brother?"

"Yeah, I get that, but it felt more like he didn't trust or believe in me. Sometimes I think he still saw us all as little kids. Hell, I was willing to get married to prove to him I was a grown-up."

"What do you mean?"

He blinked and ran a hand through his hair as if he hadn't meant to admit this, but then said, "I'm not proud to admit it, but I doubt I'd have asked Bailey to marry me if I hadn't thought maybe it would help Dad see me as more of an adult. He was very traditional, and I got this idea in my head that if I had marital responsibilities, he'd see it as time to hand me some of the business responsibilities, as well. Don't get me wrong—I like Bailey and we had fun together, but there wasn't enough between us to build a lifetime. We were both going into marriage together for the wrong reasons. Thank God she saw sense."

Chelsea swallowed, uneasy at the reference to her client, but at the same time wanting to pry deeper. Was he against marriage in general? Or just marriage to Bailey?

She forced those questions from her head. "You know, I'm sure your dad is looking down from wherever he is up there and he'll see the success you make of the distillery and he'll be proud."

Callum chuckled. "I'm not sure I believe in all that 'up there' stuff, but right now he's probably turning in his grave at some of the things I'm planning to do.

"Sounds like you're going to be very busy indeed."

He winked. "Don't worry, I'll make time for you."

And then he stood and began clearing the table. As Callum carried their dishes over to the sink and started filling it with water, Chelsea watched, wondering if his feelings for her were growing at the same crazy rate as hers were for him. She refused to ask him, because if he ever confessed his love to her, she wanted him to do so of his own free will. She never wanted to feel like a burden or an obligation to anyone ever again.

She'd wondered if he might ask her to Christmas dinner with his family, but Christmas was only a week away, and he hadn't mentioned it once. It was quite obvious that turning the distillery around was his prime focus right now.

As was becoming their habit, after dinner they retreated to his bed to watch late-night television until Callum finally drifted off to sleep. Chelsea took a while to fall asleep—instead, she took the time to admire his naked form beside her. He truly was a work of art and this felt more like a relationship than anything she'd been in before. Usually when things started to head this way with a guy she was dating, she freaked and ended it, but the closer she got to Callum, the more she didn't want it to end.

After a taxing day, which included a long drive to do a face-to-face breakup in a town on the very boundary of her face-to-face region, Chelsea returned to her place exhausted. She and Callum had made no official plans to meet that evening. In fact, he hadn't sent her so much as a text message today. She guessed he was just busy with all the new plans for the distillery, but she missed the messages he often sent her, which brightened her days. And she couldn't help worrying that maybe there was more to his silence. Was he getting bored with her? This feeling of anxiousness in relation to a man was a new one and she didn't like it one bit.

Not knowing whether he'd turn up later or not, she'd bought enough Indian takeout in case he did and a big tub of their favorite ice cream for dessert. Their love of nutty coconut was another one of the many things they'd found in common.

"Muffin, come inside," Chelsea called to her dog. He was sniffing something over by the fence and eventually trundled over to her with a raw piece of meat in his hands.

"Gross," she exclaimed, leaning down to grab it out of his mouth. She hurled it toward the street, then with her unbloody hand opened the door. Muffin skulked off to the kitchen, obviously angry at her for stealing his treasure. Chelsea followed, dumped the takeout on the counter and the ice cream in the freezer and then went into her bedroom to change into more comfortable clothes.

She'd taken two steps into her bedroom, when the door slammed shut behind her. Frowning, she looked to the window, wondering if she'd left it open and the breeze had blown the door shut, and then her heart thudded in her chest at the sight of broken glass. Someone had thrown a brick into her house; it now lay in the pile of shattered glass on her bedroom floor.

"Hello, Chelsea," said a menacing voice, and she spun around to come face-to-face with a man she vaguely recognized. He smiled creepily at her and she suddenly placed him as a guy she'd dumped a few months back. A man who'd been on the list she'd given the police of people who could potentially bear a grudge against her, but who, like all the others, had been ruled out as dangerous. She remembered his girlfriend had cited his neediness as one of the main reasons for the breakup.

"Finally I have your attention," said the guy.

Her whole body trembling, Chelsea somehow managed to say, "Freddie, isn't it? What are you doing here?"

"You hurt me" was his reply and she swallowed, not knowing how to respond. "I loved Lara and *you* split us up."

On the other side of the closed door, Muffin started barking like a crazy dog and Chelsea silently prayed her elderly neighbor Maureen didn't have her television turned up too loud and would hear him.

"Did you leave that piece of meat out front for my dog?" she asked, her tone equally as accusing as his.

Her heart turned icy as she wondered exactly what this lovelorn man was capable of. "Was it poisoned?"

"It wouldn't have killed him, just made him sick. I'm not an animal hurter. I just…"

His voice trailed off and, hoping her words wouldn't aggravate him further, Chelsea changed her form of attack. "I'm sorry you've been hurting," she began. Her spray deodorant was only an arm's length away from her on the dresser. If she could grab it without him seeing, then she could spray him in the eyes, which would hopefully stun him enough to give her time to escape.

"My life isn't worth living without Lara in it," Freddie said, his unnerving gaze on her never wavering. "Since you told me it was over, she won't take my calls or see me. How am I supposed to win her back if she won't even talk to me?"

You're not. That's the whole idea of breaking up. Of course Chelsea knew better than to say this to him.

"Do you want my help? Is that why you've been calling me?" she asked.

Freddie blinked, as if wondering whether to admit to this or not. Then he said, "Yes. But also to make you stop doing what you're doing. You're going to hurt other men too. But you didn't listen. You didn't stop. Even after I broke into your house a few weeks back and left poo on your porch yesterday, you still keep dumping men like me. I've seen you."

She failed to see how she was supposed to get his message from a pile of horse manure, but that didn't matter now. What mattered was that he knew about the breakups she'd done lately and had all but confessed to following her. So she hadn't been imagining it after all. This thought brought little comfort, and she glanced again at the deodorant. "If you'd left a message instead of hanging up all the time, I could have talked to you, Freddie. We could have worked something out."

"It's not *my* fault you do what you do!" he shouted, spittle shooting from his mouth.

"I didn't say it was," she said, taking the tiniest of steps toward her dresser. The way he shouted at her, reminded her of the way her dad had shouted at her and her mom whenever he was drunk. It was hard to tell if Freddie was an actual threat or just a really sad guy, but as he'd broken into her house twice and tried to poison her dog, she decided to take him seriously. "You seem like a great guy. Lara has obviously made a terrible mistake."

"Thanks to you," he spat, as she took another almost imperceptible step.

"Yes, thanks to me," she agreed, her palms so sweaty she could feel the perspiration running down them. "Tell me about your relationship with Lara. What is so special about her?" If she could get him talking, maybe she could make him see that the breakup was a good thing. At the least, it would hopefully distract him so he wouldn't notice her dive for the deodorant.

Freddie stared at her a moment as if trying to work out if this were a trick question, then his stance relaxed a little and he started to talk. He told her about how Lara and he met at a soup kitchen where they both cooked for the homeless and how she was the kindest, prettiest girl he ever knew. He told her of dates they'd been on and how he wanted to move in together but she'd thought it was too soon.

"She sounds very special," Chelsea agreed, "but you know what? All those romantic dates you planned show that you're a pretty amazing guy yourself. You deserve someone who really appreciates all that, and it doesn't sound like Lara is that girl. I know you're hurting—losing someone you love is the worst feeling ever—but if you accept Lara's decision and let her go, I believe there's someone even better out there waiting for you."

She knew these words were risky and couldn't imagine any woman wanting a man who would break in and trash another woman's apartment, but there was some truth in her message.

Finally, with his head cocked to one side, Freddie spoke, "You are kinder than I imagined." He sighed and wrung his hands together. "I'm sorry. I'm not really a bad dude, I can't believe I—"

At that moment the door behind him burst open and Callum exploded into the room, his nostrils flared and his eyes cold as he launched at Freddie, grabbing hold of him and yanking his arms behind his back so he couldn't move.

Chelsea let out a long breath she hadn't realized she'd been holding as Muffin jumped up at Freddie's knees, barking louder than he ever had before.

"Are you okay?" Callum looked to her, speaking over the top of Freddie's head.

She nodded, blinking back the tears that threatened now that the danger was over.

Callum turned his attention to Freddie. "Who the hell are you? And what do you think you're doing?"

Freddie looked terrified and Chelsea's heart went out to him. He was misguided, yes, but deep down she didn't think him evil. "You're hurting him!"

Callum glared at her. "And what the hell do you think he would have done to you if I hadn't turned up when I did? Call the police!" Ignoring her, he turned back to Freddie. "Are you the one who broke into her house before? You better start talking!"

Her hands shaking and her heart still racing, Chelsea knew there was no point arguing with Callum right now. Besides, although she believed she'd almost had the situation under control, she couldn't deny the relief she'd felt when Callum had appeared like a knight in shining armor to rescue her. She staggered past the men into the kitchen, grabbed her cell from her purse and dialed 911. Part of her felt sorry for Freddie and didn't want to get him into trouble, but she hoped if he were charged for the phone calls and the break-ins maybe the authorities would get him the psychological help he needed.

Chapter Thirteen

Callum didn't let the intruder go until two uniformed police officers arrived and cuffed him. Finally, and only then, did his muscles start to relax and his breathing return to normal.

He'd arrived at Chelsea's place and heard frantic barks the moment he'd climbed out of the SUV. After a few weeks of being in Muffin's company, he'd come to identify his different barks and recognized instantly that this wasn't a good one. Although there was every chance Chelsea hadn't heard his knock on the door over the noise of the barking, when it went unanswered, Callum's hackles had risen, an uneasy feeling settling in his gut. He'd tried the door handle and, after discovering it unlocked, hesitated only a few moments before letting himself inside. The fact the little dog hadn't abandoned his pursuit to welcome

Callum only increased his anxiety. He'd stormed into the hallway and found Muffin on the wrong side of Chelsea's closed bedroom door. There was no logical reason why she would lock the dog out and that was all the encouragement he'd needed to fling open the door and barge inside.

It had taken him all of two seconds to analyze the situation—window broken, glass shattered all over the room, Chelsea over by the dresser, an oily-haired sleazy-looking man standing threateningly before her, blocking her passage to the door.

And Callum had seen red. He'd launched himself at the guy and barely managed to control the rage blustering inside him. In hindsight, he reckoned he deserved a medal for the self-control he'd displayed by *not* ripping the man's tonsils out and feeding them to Muffin for dinner.

But, thankfully, the man was now gone and the danger over. A whimpering mess when the cops questioned him, Freddie had confessed to a whole host of offenses relating to Chelsea—most of which were news to Callum. He couldn't believe that while they'd been sleeping together, she'd never thought to mention she was getting threatening phone calls and was worried about someone following her. He could have *done* something.

They stood on the porch, Muffin still barking, as they watched the police car reverse into the road. Then Callum turned to Chelsea and yanked her into his arms.

He inhaled the vanilla scent of her hair and relished her soft loveliness pressed against him. She felt so damn good, she fit so perfectly, and the thought of anything bad happening to her made him crazy.

"Move in with me," he begged.

"What?" Chelsea pulled back from his embrace and looked at him as if he were as mentally unstable as Freddie.

He was almost as surprised as her by his question, but it made sense, didn't it?

They'd been spending practically every night together anyway and after coming upon Freddie in her bedroom, Callum wouldn't ever be able to sleep soundly knowing she was home alone.

"You'll be safe with me, out at the distillery," he said, his thoughts storming ahead, "and while you're studying to do counseling, you could work with us. Sophie was only saying the other day how she's struggling with the social media side of things since taking on the extra merchandise planning and stuff."

When Chelsea simply stared at him, he continued, "You'd be great at that. You're good online since you've run your business mostly through the internet. And, the job will be flexible, so you can—"

Chelsea held up a hand to interrupt him. "Let me get this straight. You want me to move in with you and work at the distillery."

He nodded. "It makes perfect sense."

"To whom?" She took a step back and threw her hands up in the air. "I don't need your protection, Callum McKinnel. I might have been handling things differently than you would have with Freddie, but I almost had everything under control when you stormed in there all heavy-handed. And I already have a job, one I can do while I'm studying, *if*—and I haven't decided on that yet—I go the counseling route."

Her words were like venom and he couldn't understand why she was angry at him. He was only trying to help, only looking out for the woman he cared about. "Yesterday you said you were starting to question your career."

She snapped her hands to her hips and glared at him. "Well, today I'm remembering how important it is. How helping people end a relationship when those in it have different priorities, different needs and desires is a very worthwhile profession. In fact, I think it's time to tell you that this thing we have going on has met its expiration date."

"What?"

"It's over, Callum. You can stop feeling like you need to protect me from danger, because that was never what this was about. I warned you that I didn't do relationships, this was just a charade that got out of hand, so don't pretend this is a big surprise. Thanks for the fun. Merry Christmas and good luck with the distillery. I'm sure you'll make it a great success."

And with those words, Chelsea grabbed Muffin's collar and hauled herself and the dog inside. She slammed the door shut in his face, leaving him standing out on the porch in the freezing evening air wondering what the hell had just happened.

He'd been starting to think this was something real, something more than just sex between him and Chelsea, but the moment he took a step toward commitment, she'd all but thrown it in his face. He stared at the closed door for a few more moments, dithering about storming right back inside and kissing some sense into her, but she'd made her feelings perfectly clear. If he barged in and tried to plead his case, he'd be no better than Freddie, unable to accept that she didn't feel the same way about him as he did about her.

He'd sliced open his heart and bared his soul talking about his family and his hopes and dreams, but now he realized Chelsea had been very reticent about sharing much about herself. That showed exactly how she felt about their liaison. For a guy who hadn't thought he wanted a relationship right now, her rejection cut deep. Much, much deeper than his breakup with Bailey had.

It was with this thought in his head that he managed to drag himself off the porch, over to his SUV and drive slowly home where he immediately headed for the sofa to drown his sorrows in a bottle of McKinnel's finest whiskey.

"Well, that's it then." Chelsea spoke to Muffin as she peeked through her curtain to watch Callum's SUV disappear into the night. "I've done it again, although for a different reason than usual." She sounded far more nonchalant than she felt, but despite the aching in her heart, which was growing by the second, ending things with Callum was the right thing to do.

While she'd been fantasizing about him offering her more than the no-strings fun they'd been enjoying, he'd only asked her to move in with him out of a perverted sense of duty. And that was the last thing she wanted. She'd spent her childhood and most of her adolescence with people who'd felt obliged to look after her and no way was she going down that path again as an adult.

She had too much self-respect for that and as much as her heart might hate her right now, in time it would recover and so would she. She was the breakup expert after all—she knew all the tricks for recovering from a broken heart, even if she'd never actually had one herself. Until now.

"First step ice cream."

Muffin barked his approval, then tottered after her into the kitchen.

Ignoring the scents of India wafting from the take-out bag on the counter, she went straight to the freezer, retrieved the ice cream she'd bought for their dessert and then grabbed a spoon to eat it with. She took these things to the couch, switched on the TV, peeled off the lid and then dug her spoon right in. But when the first spoonful melted on her tongue, it didn't offer any of the comfort she'd been hoping for. This ice cream, which she'd now shared with Callum numerous times, tasted like their late-night kisses.

A tear slipping down her cheek, Chelsea dumped the ice cream—spoon and all—on the coffee table in front of her. Had he broken her heart *and* ruined her favorite ice cream for her? She didn't think she'd ever be able to enjoy nutty coconut again. She swiped at the tear, but it was no good as another one replaced it almost immediately. Then another and another and another until she found herself curled in the fetal position on her sofa bawling her eyes out.

Every inch of her ached, as if the pain was seeping from her broken heart and spreading like wildfire through her body. She started to shake and Muffin came up beside her and shoved his head into her face, licking the salt from her cheeks. She pulled him into her arms, seeking the comfort his warm, furry body had always given, but this time it didn't work.

Yes, she still had Muffin, but he was no longer enough. She wanted Callum more than she'd wanted her parents to stop drinking when she was a child, and she wanted *him* to want *her* with that same desperation.

Taking a deep breath, Chelsea tried to imagine sitting across a table from herself—what would her professional persona say to her right now? She thought of her words to Freddie earlier in the evening but, now that she was in his position, they felt empty and she could understand why he'd acted the way he did. Love messed with your brain, it made you think crazy thoughts and want to do crazy things. No wonder it was sometimes referred to as a drug.

In her two years of being the breakup girl, she'd handed out numerous pieces of advice on how to recover. Aside from the ice cream, there were many practical steps one could take in this process.

Find your independence again. How many people had she encouraged to go pursue a new hobby or interest in order to distract them from their hurt? She thought of her hobby—jigsaws—and let out a gut-wrenching sob. They'd never be the same again either.

Help someone. This involved donating your time to a good cause—like helping out at a homeless shelter or something. The idea being that helping someone else through hardship might help you forget yours or realize it's not as bad as you think.

Get out of the house and meet new people—you'll soon learn there truly are more fish in the sea. Or simply get online and do so.

As Chelsea ticked through all the steps in her head, she stumbled across one major problem. Right now, she didn't know how she'd ever be able to summon the will to leave her couch ever again and, unfortunately, moving on required effort.

Maybe she should have said yes. Callum wouldn't have asked her to move in with him if he didn't at least like her, and like could turn to love, couldn't it? If she'd said yes, right now she'd be in his arms and they'd be…

Jeez, listen to yourself. The nostalgic voice in her head sounded exactly like the kind of desperate she despised. How the heck had one man made such an imprint on her life, on *her*, in such a short time?

She'd fallen hard and fast, and now her only hope was that the time needed to get over him was equally as short.

Chapter Fourteen

Callum stared at the range of sample merchandise Sophie had spread over his desk and tried to feign some kind of enthusiasm. As she rattled on about each item and how it would work to enhance their new image, he rubbed a hand against his forehead, wishing like hell his damn headache would take a hike. He'd drunk too much last night. Hell, he'd drunk too much every night since Chelsea had dumped him. Always with the aim to obliterate thoughts of her—it worked to an extent for a fraction of a time, but in the mornings he always regretted it.

If he wasn't careful he'd be sliding down the same slippery slope he worried about Mac traveling, and after all those conversations about Chelsea's parents, he should know better. He needed to get a grip or all his innovative ideas for the distillery were going to be ruined in the aftermath of his self-destruction.

It was time to find another vice. He'd thought work enough but...

"And this," Sophie said, pointing to a little box with a postcard-perfect image of the distillery printed on the top, "is quite possibly my favorite product."

Positively beaming, she lifted the box, removed the lid and upturned it. He watched in horror as what looked like hundreds of little pieces of card fell onto his desk, scattering across everything else.

"What the hell is that?"

Sophie half frowned, half smirked. "It's a puzzle, brother dear. They're very popular at the moment believe it or not. They're experiencing some sort of resurgence, a bit like adult coloring books, which I also think we should consider selling—McKinnel branded of course. A guy Storie knows has started up this company in Bend, creating high quality, personalized gifts and he can do these puzzles for us at an awesome price."

Callum heard nothing of what she said—glancing down at all the puzzle pieces, his heart squeezed so hard he was certain he was having a heart attack. Whatever he did, wherever he went, there were reminders of Chelsea and they were suffocating him. He pushed back his office chair, opened his desk drawer and grabbed his car keys.

"I need some fresh air" was all the excuse he gave his sister as he strode past her and out of his office. He barely registered the customers milling around the tasting room or Mac and Lachlan outside starting to take measurements for the restaurant extensions—all he could think about was his escape.

He crunched over the frosty ground to his SUV,

climbed inside and then he drove, having no destination in mind, simply needing to get away from the distillery and from the memories. Less than a month he'd known Chelsea and now wherever he looked there were memories of her—in his house, in the distillery, even in his goddamn office where they'd laughed their heads off together as they'd erased the footage of their naughty night.

Callum drove aimlessly—or so he thought—until he found himself slowing in front of the animal shelter where he'd rescued Muffin. He recalled his thought to get a dog a few weeks back and it made more sense now. A dog would make his house less empty when he stepped inside, and taking it for runs would be a better way to spend his spare time than staring into a bottle of bourbon. Besides, he'd gotten used to having a dog around the last few weeks. And he'd liked it.

His decision made, he parked his vehicle and as he strode toward the building, he felt a sense of déjà vu. The little bell above the door ding-donged as he stepped inside and he inhaled the scent of disinfectant mixed with animal smells. As he crossed over to the counter, he passed by the row of cages holding cats and paid no attention whatsoever until a paw stretched out and some claws snagged on his woolen sweater. Frowning, he stopped and turned to see a mammoth ginger cat peering at him with big, pleading, green eyes. It let out a long meow, which sounded so sad it shot right to Callum's heart.

"Hi there, how can I help you?" An elderly woman, her clothes covered in animal fur, appeared beside him. "You seem to have made friends with Bourbon. Would you like to know more about him?"

He shook his arm free of the cat. "Bourbon?"

The woman smiled warmly. "That's what we named the ginger cat. Are you looking for a new feline friend?"

"Definitely not." No matter what the cat was called, he was in the market for a dog. "Have you got any German shepherds?"

"We're a refuge shelter, sir," she said, narrowing her eyes at him and crossing her arms over her large bosom. "If you're looking for a purebred—"

"I'm not," he interrupted, setting her straight. "I'm just looking for a dog who needs a lot of exercise. I want a friend and a running partner."

The lines around her eyes softened again as she smiled. "I'm not sure we have anything that fits your bill exactly, but we do have a lot of lovely dogs. Come and have a look."

He followed her through a door, down a corridor and past rows and rows of cages filled with more cats. It was like an animal prison.

"Why is the ginger cat out front?" he asked, racking his head for anyone else he knew who could do with the company of a pet.

"Bourbon?" She sighed. "He's been with us a long time. We rotate the animals in the foyer so they're always ones in dire need of a new home."

"Right." Callum ignored what felt like barbed wire twisting around his heart and followed her outside to even more cages. The noise of yapping dogs assaulted him, yet after doing two rounds of the canine yard, he hadn't found any animal that met his requirements. Most of the pups available barely stood taller than his ankle and no way in hell was he getting a dog that would fit in a purse. He might end up stepping on it in the dark.

"I'm going to need to think about this some more," he said.

"Of course." Although the woman smiled at him, her shoulders sagged and the sparkle left her eyes. "I'll see you out."

Chelsea had lived on her own a long time and had become accustomed to quiet nights in; in fact, she loved nothing more than coming home at night, cooking herself some dinner and relaxing in front of the TV with a jigsaw puzzle to stimulate her mind and Muffin warming her feet.

Loved as in past tense.

It had been a matter of days since she'd said goodbye to Callum for the final time and now she dreaded coming home at night almost as much as she dreaded leaving the house for work. She'd done two face-to-face breakups in that time and made a total botch of both of them. One poor guy had ended up comforting her when she'd burst into tears while telling him his girlfriend didn't want him anymore. She felt other people's pain more strongly than she ever had before.

Her little house no longer filled her with joy and a sense of achievement. Muffin, still his energetic adorable self, no longer satisfied her craving for company. It was Christmas in a few days and the prospect of spending it alone left her cold. She was desperately close to falling into a black funk that would be almost impossible to climb out of. Nothing she could think to do felt like it would cure her. She couldn't even summon the enthusiasm to put up a Christmas tree when no one but she and Muffin would see it.

Finally, deciding it was unhealthy to spend the holidays alone in her little house, she called Rosie in Portland to ask if she could visit.

"Long time no speak," Rosie said when she answered the phone in her usual jovial tone. She was such a vivacious soul and Chelsea only hoped a few days with her friend would be the boost she needed.

"Sorry, I've been busy with work." It wasn't a lie. The breakup business was booming—unfortunately she found no solace from the fact that hers was only one of hundreds of broken hearts floating around.

"What's wrong?" Rosie's tone turned serious and Chelsea's grip tightened on her cell.

"Nothing," she said, trying to sound like she meant it.

"I know you and I can tell from your voice that this isn't just a friendly catch-up. What's the matter?"

"How do you *do* that?" Chelsea asked.

"It's a talent. I have a sixth sense where my best friends are concerned."

So Chelsea hit her with it: "I've fallen in love." This announcement was met with protracted silence. "Are you still there?" she asked eventually.

"Yes. Sorry. Just give me a second to pick my jaw back up off the floor."

At Rosie's words, Chelsea almost smiled, which proved that some friend therapy was exactly what the doctor ordered.

"So let me get this straight," Rosie said. "You have met a guy you still want to be with after a few months?"

"Yes. Well, it hasn't even been a month yet but…it's

different this time." Chelsea sniffed as she tried to fight the tears that threatened at this confession.

"Oh. My. Freaking. God! Tell me all about him. Who is this man of men? When do I get to meet him?"

"That's just it," Chelsea admitted, "I dumped him." And then she succumbed to more tears.

Callum stared at the cat, who had made itself at home from almost the moment he let it out of its box and now sat on the kitchen table, surveying the sights around him as if he were a king. He'd totally lost his head thinking that a cat could fill the void Chelsea had left in his life. He guess this proved his worst fear—he hadn't been with her because he was lonely, he'd been with her because he didn't want to be without her.

"At least you have a cool name," Callum said, reaching out and rubbing Bourbon under the chin. In adopting a fat cat instead of a manly dog, he'd basically given his brothers an open invitation to tease him for the rest of his days. He could hear them now—*Callum the crazy cat lady*—but he didn't care. That would take effort. And, although he'd gone out today to get a pet in the hopes that it would distract him from his continuous thoughts of Chelsea, it hadn't worked.

And thinking about her all the time was simply exhausting.

He turned back to his laptop screen and tried to exorcise her from his mind for the hundredth time that evening.

A knock sounded on his front door and he groaned. "Shh," he told Bourbon. "If we're very quiet, maybe they'll go away." He guessed it might be Sophie come to confront him about his weird behavior today and, although he owed her an apology for running out, he couldn't face that right now.

Instead, it was his mom, which was far, far worse. Her knock was merely a formality and two seconds later she let herself into the house. "Callum!" she called as her boots click-clacked along the corridor toward him. "It's Mom. Are you in here?" He closed his eyes and wished he'd thought to lock the door.

"No," he shouted. "Go away."

She appeared in the doorway and frowned at him. "That's no way to speak to your poor old mother. Sophie warned me you were in a mood. What's going—" Her question died on her tongue as her eyes came to rest on Bourbon.

"Is that a cat?"

"No, Mom, it's a horse." It appeared his wounded heart amplified his tendency toward sarcasm, but she ignored this and crossed to the feline, stooping down to stroke him.

"Hello, gorgeous girl," she cooed as she scratched under his chin.

"*He's* a boy," Callum said, although judging by the sound of Bourbon's purrs, he wasn't too fussy about little things like gender.

Nora looked back to Callum. "I do like him, but if you're hoping he'll fill the hole in your heart left by Chelsea, I think you'll be sadly disappointed."

"What?" he scoffed, instinctively glancing down at his chest, almost expecting to see a gory wound there.

She smiled tenderly at him. "I should have realized that you and Bailey weren't marriage material because being near her didn't light up your whole face the way Chelsea did when you sat beside her at Thanksgiving.

I'm sorry if I pushed you into that. And I know you don't think you have time for a relationship—I admire your dedication and commitment to McKinnel's—but..." She paused and cleared her throat. "I don't want you to make the same mistakes your father did."

"Huh?" Callum frowned at her—that wasn't the direction he'd been expecting.

"I loved your father," Nora said, "but he was single-minded. He did love us in his own way, but the distillery was all that ever mattered to him. I'm not sure, in the end, if it made him as happy as he wanted us to believe."

"What?" His mom's words stunned him. It was the first time in all his life he'd ever considered that his parents hadn't had the perfect relationship.

"I want you to have more in your life than work," she continued. "Was that the problem with Chelsea? You didn't think you had room for her?"

He shook his head and found himself confessing everything. "Maybe at first I didn't think I had time for a real relationship, but I guess I'm not quite as driven as Dad was because Chelsea got under my skin in a way I never imagined. And now, no matter how much I try to focus on work, I can't forget her."

"So what happened then? Why are you sitting here alone with a big, gorgeous furball when you should be with her?"

"My feelings weren't reciprocated. She dumped me," he confessed. "That's two times in a month—I guess I'm not much of a catch after all."

His mom frowned and then sat down at the table, all the while tickling Bourbon under the chin. "Tell me everything, sweetheart."

And the way she looked at him had Callum opening up like he hadn't done since he was a kid with a scraped knee sobbing for his mom to make things better. He told her about Chelsea's work, the way they really met and about Freddie and his threats. And how seeing her in danger made everything real for him.

"You love her." It was a statement more than a question.

"Yes." He nodded—it was the first time he'd admitted it to himself, never mind anyone else. It was the only explanation for the way she made him feel. "More than I thought I ever could."

"And did you tell her that?"

He ran a hand through his hair. "Not in so many words, but I asked her to move in with me; if that didn't make my feelings pretty damn obvious, I don't know what will."

"Callum, Callum, Callum." She sighed. "Women need to hear the words. And from what you've just told me, she probably thought your invitation to move in was a reaction to her break-in. Women don't want…"

And suddenly something clicked into place inside his head.

He didn't know about women, but he knew about Chelsea! Hadn't she told him about the burden she'd been for most of her childhood? His heart had broken every time she let down her guard long enough to talk about her past, about how it felt to be passed from one unwilling family member to the next. Yet he'd gone and made her feel the way she never wanted to feel again— asking her to move in with him in a way that made it feel like a reaction to the break-in. Yes, the burglary had instigated his question, but the moment he'd asked her to share his home, he'd known he wanted to share everything with her. His home, his life, their pets and one day children. He loved her—with absolutely everything he had to give—and deep down, he thought she loved him too.

He didn't blame her for saying no to the way he'd asked, but why-oh-why had he ever taken no for an answer? He didn't accept no easily where the distillery was concerned, and Chelsea meant even more to him than it did. He should have made her listen. He should have made her see the truth.

An idea started to take form inside his head.

As if his mom could read his mind, a warm, encouraging smile spread across her face. "Why the hell are you still sitting here pining for her like a wounded teenager? Grow some balls, go be a man and tell that girl how you feel."

"I will," he promised, "but first I have to arrange a few things." This time when he asked her to be with him, he was going to give her an offer too good to refuse. And he was going to make exactly what he wanted clear, and what he wanted was Chelsea.

He reached across the table, picked up his cell and phoned his sister. "I'm sorry about today," he said the moment Sophie answered the phone; he continued on before she had a chance to accept his apology. "But I need your help. You know that guy who makes the jigsaw puzzles? How long does it take for him to design and make them?"

Chapter Fifteen

As Chelsea headed for the front door, Muffin ran ahead and started barking like a crazy dog. Since she'd been taking him with her everywhere, he'd become almost uncontrollably excitable whenever she prepared to leave the house. She chuckled at his antics, thankful she still had him for company.

"Settle down," she said as she opened the door.

Standing on her porch, his hand raised as if he'd been about to ring the bell, was the reason for Muffin's noise. The reason for her melancholy. The dog leaped at Callum as if it had been years rather than days since they'd seen each other and Chelsea's heart leaped into her throat. She felt a tad put out that Muffin was no longer content with just her company, but seemed to have missed Callum as much as she had.

"Hey, buddy," he said, dropping to his haunches to give the dog the attention it craved.

Chelsea took the opportunity to pull herself together, to try to slow the erratic racing of her heart and, if she were honest, to soak up his gorgeousness just a little. She'd thought she would never see that beautiful face and body again and now here he was, standing on her porch on Christmas Eve, and well, she couldn't waste the opportunity.

"What are you doing here?" she asked, self-protection kicking in. Perhaps he'd left something here. Although she was pretty certain if he had, she'd have seen it by now.

Callum straightened and it was then that she noticed the small gift-wrapped box in his hands. "I got this for you." He held it out to her but she didn't take it.

"Why?" she asked, glaring at it like it were a bomb about to explode. What was he playing at? If this was some kind of let's-still-be-friends gift, he could shove it where the sun didn't shine. Then again, what if it was some kind of attempt at making amends? What if he were here to ask her out again? Her heart kicked a little at this thought.

"You'll see when you open it. *Please*, open it."

"I'm on my way out. To Portland. To go stay with Rosie." She didn't know why she was telling him all this; after all, she didn't owe him an itinerary, but she felt the need to fill the space between them with words.

"Please," he said again, and something in his eyes made her heart slow a little. "It won't take long."

Against her better judgment, she stepped aside and gestured for him to come on in. She took the box, dumped her luggage, then marched into the kitchen and laid his gift on the counter. Her fingers shook as she opened it, and the way he stood there watching only made her more nervous. Beneath the wrapping was a plain brown box. Curious, she lifted the lid to discover it was filled with puzzle pieces.

She glanced over at Callum and he nodded at the box. "Would you do it for me?"

"Now?" This visit was getting weirder by the second.

He nodded. "It's important, please."

She squeezed her eyes shut and felt her resolve wavering. There weren't that many pieces so it wouldn't take her long to do, and she wouldn't be that late getting to Portland. Call her a sucker for punishment but a few moments with Callum could be her Christmas present to herself. Yep, she was a sad case if ever there was one.

"Okay." She opened her eyes again. "But where's the image?"

"There isn't one. But a puzzle pro like yourself should be able to handle it, right?"

Never one to resist a challenge like that, she began to sort the outer pieces—all those with straight edges. In spite of the company, the buzz of doing a puzzle kicked through her veins and she had to admit she was curious about what she'd find when she'd put it all together.

"Are you going to help?" she asked, when she'd completed the border and Callum hadn't moved an inch.

He shook his head. "I'll leave this to the experts. In fact, why don't I take Muffin outside for a bit of exercise while you do it?"

Chelsea frowned, totally perplexed by his odd behavior. "Okay, whatever." This situation was so bizarre that she'd welcome a few moments' reprieve from his intoxicating proximity.

You could have just told him to take a hike, said a voice in her head. She ignored it because, however needy and desperate it made her, she'd been happy to see him. Hope that maybe they could pick off where they'd left off, but take things slower this time, filled her heart.

Callum grabbed Muffin's lead and promised to be back soon. Chelsea sent a quick message to Rosie saying she'd been delayed and then returned to the puzzle, which was starting to take form and appeared to be mostly some kind of writing. Like a newspaper's masthead. The word *missing* appeared. Then *my*. As the puzzle neared completion, Chelsea's fingers began to shake again—the words had to mean something, there had to be a message. Frantically she fit one piece after another so that within a few more moments she could read it.

Every cell in her body froze as she eyed the words on the counter in front of her: *You're the missing piece of my puzzle.*

There were footsteps behind her and she turned to see Muffin and Callum had returned. He dropped to one knee and she sucked in a breath, her hand rushing to cover her mouth.

"You're the missing piece of me," he said, his eyes and tone earnest as he repeated the sentiment on the puzzle. "Please, marry me, and make me whole."

Chelsea's head spun as his words ricocheted around it.

"Marry you?" she finally managed to whisper. Was this some kind of dream?

He nodded. "I know you think I asked you to move in with me because of the break-in, and there might be a smidgen of truth in that, but the rest of the truth is that in a few short weeks you've become as much a part of me as breathing is. I can no more live without you than I can without my lungs."

She grabbed hold of the countertop, feeling as if she might faint at any moment.

"Until you came along," he said, "I didn't realize that I wanted more out of life. I thought a good career and a relationship based on a solid friendship was all I needed, but you've shown me how much more life has to offer if you open up your heart. I've only ever proposed to two women in my life—the first time was for all the wrong reasons, but this time I'm asking because I truly mean it. I want you to be my wife more than anything."

"Those are beautiful words," she whispered, her voice shaking like a leaf on a stormy day. "You're quite the romantic, you know."

Of course, she couldn't bring herself to believe him. She must have fallen asleep while packing. This Callum standing in front of her, offering himself as her husband, had to be a figment of her imagination.

"Trust me, I wasn't the slightest bit romantic until you," said the illusion. "You've brought out a lot of things in me. Hell, because of you, I even got a cat."

Muffin's ears perked up at the word *cat*—who said dog's weren't smart?—but Chelsea shook her head. Yep—he was speaking gobbledygook—this was a dream indeed. Still, she persisted in talking to him. "You've lost me. You got a cat? What's that got to do with me?"

He sighed and shifted as if it was getting uncomfortable down there on one knee. "It's a long story. I was lonely without you, so I went to get a dog and ended up with a big, ginger, tomcat named Bourbon, so I think it's only fair that you become co-owner. A single man with a cat gives off the wrong kind of vibe, but a couple with a cat, that's perfect acceptable. Anyway I'm sure you'll love him."

She blinked, struggling to keep up, and Callum smiled up at her. "So what do you say? Will you marry me? Because my knee's going numb down here and if you're going to break my heart by saying no, then you may as well get it over with."

She blinked again. "Oh my God, you're serious?" So much for taking things slower. She could never in her wildest imaginings have come up with this.

He turned and gestured to Muffin's collar. "I wouldn't have bought this if I wasn't."

Following his hand, Chelsea's eyes caught on something glistening on the dog's collar. Her jaw dropped as she peered closer to see a beautiful diamond ring dangling next to his dog tag. It was a white-gold setting with a large square-cut diamond, surrounded by lots of smaller ones. Muffin looked proud to have been charged with its care. She'd never seen anything as stunning. Her ring finger twitched.

"I took Muffin outside and we had a man-to-man chat," Callum explained. "He wants you to know you'll make us both very happy if you just say yes. I love you, Chelsea. I think I started falling in love with you that day you walked into the distillery and tried to break my heart."

A half laugh, half sob escaped her mouth at the absurdity of his words. "Say it again," she asked, wanting to be sure her ears weren't playing evil tricks.

His lips curled into a slow, sexy smile. "What? That I love you?"

"Yes, that." A tear slid down her cheek—no one had ever said they loved her before, not in a way that made her believe it anyway. And the most wonderful thing of all was that she felt exactly the same way.

"Oh, Callum." Her words choked, she rushed forward and dropped to her knees in front of him. "Yes, I'll marry you. I love you too. I've missed you so much. I didn't think—"

Callum's need to kiss her overcame the need to hear the rest of her sentence. Nothing else mattered except the fact she loved him too and soon she'd be wearing his ring. He cupped her face in his hands and drew his lips to hers, never ever wanting to let her go again. The past few weeks had been a whirlwind but they'd held the best moments of his life and it was all because of her.

He couldn't wait to make more memories and a whole host of plans for the future, but right now having her in his arms was enough.

After what might have been one of the longest lip-locks in history, Muffin's bark broke them apart. Laughing, they looked sideways to see the dog watching them, his head cocked to one side like a confused puppy.

Callum reached over and ruffled Muffin's fur, then he unclipped his collar and removed the ring he'd spent hours choosing today while Sophie's acquaintance had done a rush job on the puzzle for him.

"I hope you like it," he said as he lifted her hand and slipped the ring onto her finger. It sparkled as they both gazed down at it.

"Like it?" She wiggled her fingers and giggled. "I love it. You have very good taste, you know that?"

"Of course I do. I chose you, didn't I?"

"Yes, you did," she whispered, and then she said, "Can you pinch me?"

He frowned. "What for?"

"So I can know this is real."

"It's real, sweetheart. Nothing has ever been as real as this, so how about I just kiss you again instead?"

And he did.

Epilogue

Chelsea stared at the little white stick in her hand, almost unable to believe the two blue lines looking up at her. *Pregnant.* The last few days she'd noticed changes in her body but didn't dare hope too much that this was what they meant, so she'd kept her suspicions to herself until she could get into town to buy a test kit.

She and Callum were getting married in spring—they were going to be the first couple to use the distillery grounds as a venue, Lachlan had planned an amazing menu to showcase the new restaurant, and she'd picked out the most beautiful dress imaginable. It was ice-pink and far more girly and princess-like than she'd ever thought she'd choose, but Callum brought out the feminine side of her and she couldn't wait to see the look on his face when he saw her. Then, in private, later in the evening, he would slowly peel it off and…

Her cheeks heating at this thought, Chelsea glanced

in the bathroom mirror and palmed her hands against her flat stomach, something glowing inside her at the thought of the tiny life beneath them. A life that she and Callum had created out of their love. She never thought she could be so lucky. So blessed.

Would she be showing by the wedding? Would the dressmaker have to alter her dress? Whatever. She didn't care. This was wonderful news and she racked her mind for the perfect way to break the news to Callum. Maybe she could have a personalized jigsaw puzzle made like he'd done when he'd proposed, although that would take time and she knew she wouldn't be able to keep this secret long enough. Right now, she felt like going outside, spreading her arms wide and shouting her news to the whole world.

While they hadn't been trying for this baby, they hadn't exactly been not trying for it either and they both wanted children. In the past few months, she'd fallen in love with the McKinnels almost as much as she had with Callum. *Almost.* Sophie and Annabel were going to be her bridesmaids alongside Rosie who had yet to meet the McKinnels but was coming for the wedding. All Callum's brothers were going to be groomsmen.

Finally Chelsea was part of a big, happy family— the kind of family she'd always fantasized about—and the news that she'd soon be adding to the McKinnel clan filled her with warm fuzzy glee.

A bark coming from the living room interrupted her happy thoughts, so she put the pregnancy test down on the vanity and went out to investigate. Sure enough, she found Muffin beside the coffee table, nose to the ground trying to entice Bourbon, who was hiding under there, out to play. The cat made low mewling noises and occasionally stretched out his paw, claws readied, and took a swipe at Muffin.

"Leave Bourbon alone," Chelsea warned, stooping to take hold of Muffin's collar and encourage him to back up. The poor dog only wanted to play and had been trying to win Bourbon's affections since he and Chelsea had moved into Callum's cottage a couple of months ago, but she feared Muffin was fighting a lost cause. Whenever he got within an inch of the cat, Bourbon narrowed his eyes and looked as if he wanted to scratch the dog's eyes right out. It was surprising there hadn't been any blood spilled yet, but they had the local vet on speed dial just in case.

As she was trying to separate the animals, the front door opened and Callum strode in, sleeves pushed up to the elbows just the way she liked them. "Hey, gorgeous," he said.

"I didn't expect you home this early." Her heart leaped into her throat at the thought of him going into the bathroom and seeing the test. She wanted to tell him. She wanted to see the look on his face when he found out he was going to be a dad.

"Sorry, did I interrupt your studying? This is just a quick visit. Truth is, I couldn't wait till tonight to do this." With those words, he crossed the room and pulled her up into his arms. She let go of Muffin's collar and, as Callum kissed her, the dog returned to his pursuit of the cat.

"These two fighting like cats and dogs again?" Callum asked when he finally tore his mouth from hers.

She rolled her eyes at his lame humor, but couldn't help smiling. He could tell the world's most awful joke and she'd still laugh her head off.

"They'll get used to each other eventually," he said, "and I suppose it's good practice for when we have kids. My brothers and I used to bicker so much I'm quite surprised we didn't kill each other."

"About kids," Chelsea began, thinking that now was as good a time as ever. She mightn't have come up with some dramatic, exciting way to tell him, but then again, this news was dramatic and exciting enough in itself.

"Yes?" He stared down at her. "What about them?"

She placed a hand on her stomach again and smiled. "In two years' time Muffin isn't the only problem Bourbon is going to have—he'll also have a toddler trying to chase his tail."

It took a moment for Callum to register what she meant. She watched, amused, as his expression changed in slow motion from confusion to one of absolute joy. Then he grabbed hold of her again and met her gaze. "Are you saying what I think you're saying?"

She nodded. "I'm pregnant. The evidence is in the bathroom if you don't believe me."

In reply, he leaned forward and kissed her again. There was just as much heat, just as much passion, as before, but there was also something else in it. Something Chelsea couldn't describe but liked very much indeed.

"Mom is going to be over the moon," he said, pulling back.

"What about you?" she asked. "Are you…over the moon?"

"Sweetheart, my darling…" He cupped her face in both his hands. "I'm so high I've gone way past the moon. This is the best news I've heard all… Ever. We're going to be parents."

"We are."

"You know, I've heard a rumor that a woman's sex drive increases when she's pregnant," Callum said, his expression suddenly serious. "I wonder if this is true?"

Chelsea rubbed her lips together and wriggled her eyebrows at him. "Hmm…perhaps that accounts for why I suddenly have an urge to strip you of all your clothes and have my wicked way."

Callum grinned and held his hands out in surrender. "Who am I to stand in the way of a pregnant woman's needs? I'm all yours, baby."

Never had any words been sweeter. "And I'm all yours too." Chelsea reached up and sealed this promise with a kiss.

* * * * *

Watch for Rachael Johns's next book in the
MCKINNELS OF JEWELL ROCK *series*
coming in March 2017 from
Mills & Boon Cherish

MILLS & BOON®

Cherish™

EXPERIENCE THE ULTIMATE RUSH OF FALLING IN LOVE

A sneak peek at next month's titles...

In stores from 11th August 2016:

- **Stepping Into The Prince's World** – Marion Lenno*
  and **A Maverick and a Half** – Marie Ferrarella
- **Unveiling The Bridesmaid** – Jessica Gilmore *and*
  A Camden's Baby Secret – Victoria Pade

In stores from 25th August 2016:

- **The CEO's Surprise Family** – Teresa Carpenter *an*
  A Word with the Bachelor – Teresa Southwick
- **The Billionaire From Her Past** – Leah Ashton *and*
  Meet Me at the Chapel – Joanna Sims

Available at WHSmith, Tesco, Asda, Eason, Amazon and Apple

Just can't wait?
Buy our books online a month before they hit the shops!
visit www.millsandboon.co.uk

These books are also available in eBook format!

0816/23

MILLS & BOON®
The Regency Collection – Part 1

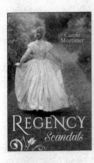

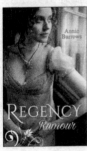

Let these roguish rakes sweep you off to the Regency period in part 1 of our collection!

Order yours at **www.millsandboon.co.uk/regency1**

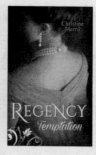